D1783771

THE LYNX WHO PURRED FOR A SIDHE PRINCE

Mate or Meal 9

Scarlet Hyacinth

EROTIC ROMANCE
MANLOVE

Siren Publishing, Inc.
www.SirenPublishing.com

A SIREN PUBLISHING BOOK
IMPRINT: Erotic Romance ManLove

THE LYNX WHO PURRED FOR A SIDHE PRINCE
Copyright © 2012 by Scarlet Hyacinth

ISBN: 978-1-62241-319-5

First Printing: September 2012

Cover design by Jinger Heaston
All cover art and logo copyright © 2012 by Siren Publishing, Inc.

Printed in the U.S.A.

PUBLISHER
Siren Publishing, Inc.
www.SirenPublishing.com

DEDICATION

To all those who commented on the new magical-creature shifter pairings. I'm glad you liked this twist. It was unexpected for me, too, but I'm having a lot of fun writing the books. Thank you all!

THE LYNX WHO PURRED FOR A SIDHE PRINCE

Mate or Meal 9

SCARLET HYACINTH
Copyright © 2012

Prologue

The sound of Winter's footsteps echoed hollowly in the cavernous halls of the Seelie palace. Winter suppressed a shudder, eyeing the guards leading him with apprehension. He had no idea what he'd done to be summoned here. Usually, his royal uncle attempted to keep him away from the court with every possible pretext. Whatever King Sterling had in store for him, it couldn't be good.

Once upon a time, Winter had loved the Sidhe palace. There were beautiful gardens where he'd loved to play as a child, and the libraries were endless sources of knowledge. During ceremonies and parties, beautiful music filled the ballrooms. Back then, Winter had been too young to participate, but he'd always sneaked as close as he could to steal a few looks at the richly garbed guests and the extravagant outfits. It had been home.

All that had changed when Winter's parents had been killed in an assassination plot by the Unseelie. After that, chaos had ensued. With the Seelie leader and his wife gone, war had been imminent. Winter had been too young to take charge of the situation and too lost in grief. This was how his uncle had ended up on the throne, even if it had been Winter's birthright.

If he wanted to be honest, Winter didn't particularly mind leaving the Seelie crown to Sterling. Being part of the royal family had only brought Winter sorrow. Many times, he had wished he'd been born in a normal household. That way, his parents wouldn't be dead now.

In spite of those regrets, however, he had not officially signed the throne over to Sterling since he knew it was not what his parents would have wanted. Winter was no politician. He preferred a more hands-on approach in helping his people. But even if what he really wanted was to be a healer, he remained the heir of the defunct royal family, the only Sidhe prince, and eventually, he would have to take up the crown.

It occurred to Winter that the palace was awfully quiet. Not only that, but there were more guards around than usual. A dark suspicion crowded at the back of his mind. He didn't want to think his uncle would plan something against him, but his parents had been assassinated after all.

"Excuse me," he said to one of the guards. "Is anything wrong? Have the Unseelie attacked again?"

The man gave Winter a torn look, as if he was considering whether to approach the topic or not. "No, Sire," he finally said. "It's nothing like that. But you should ask His Majesty for more details. I am honestly not at liberty to say."

The fact that the guards were sworn to secrecy didn't bode well for the situation. Still, Winter remained silent and obediently followed behind them. At last, they reached the throne room, and the guards stopped in front of the huge golden doors engraved with the symbol of the House of Tomacelli. Winter's family. Every time he saw that crest, Winter felt a deep pang of regret inside him.

The doors opened and one of the guards stepped forward to announce him. "His Royal Highness, Prince Winter Tomacelli."

A familiar voice beckoned him to enter, and the guards parted, allowing him to go inside. Keeping his head held high, Winter stepped into the throne room.

King Sterling was alone in the throne room, something that immediately surprised Winter. The man was always surrounded by his entourage, from courtesans to advisors. Winter carefully schooled his expression, not allowing the older Sidhe to see how much this odd situation startled him.

"Greetings, Uncle," he said. "You wanted to see me?"

Usually, it would have been a breach of protocol to address the standing Sidhe king as anything else than Your Majesty, but their current situation was unprecedented, and Winter took petty satisfaction where he could.

"Yes, Winter. Come. I wanted to talk to you about something very important."

King Sterling's voice held none of the arrogance Winter had come to expect from the other Sidhe. "Of course, Uncle," he replied neutrally.

"A few days ago, Elder Mercier was captured in an act of extreme aggression against the shifters. To prevent a war, two important shifters have come to see me. They do not wish for more violence, and I am inclined to agree."

Winter couldn't say he was particularly surprised by the information. Adele Mercier had always been one of the stoutest believers in the purist school of thought that many Seelie Sidhe had adopted. Personally, Winter believed that all species had the right to live. Sure, he knew that Elder Mercier and others like her believed shifters were to blame for the entire world knowing of the existence of paranormal creatures. Still, he'd always thought such disgust and resentment was extreme, especially since it often extended to magical creatures such as demons.

Oblivious to Winter's thoughts, Sterling continued to speak. "However, Elder Mercier's action led to the injury of several shifters, an injury of magical nature which they cannot heal."

The word *heal* truly drew in Winter's attention. He was beginning to understand where Sterling was going with this. "You want me to help them with this in a sign of good faith?"

Sterling offered him a weak smile. "Indeed. You've always been a smart boy." The small twist of lips disappeared as if it had never been. "But there's more. There is a child."

"A child?" Winter repeated, unsure if he'd heard right. What did a baby have anything to do with a war?

Sterling nodded. "He is the grandson of our two visitors and the product of a union that was, for a long time, cursed." He paused, as if for effect. "I want that child."

Winter's mind went blank. He couldn't understand what his uncle was saying. "I'm sorry. I'm not sure I get what you're trying to say."

"That baby has to be here, with me," his uncle insisted. "I will demand the child in exchange for an alliance between our peoples, but I have reason to believe that I will be denied. This is why I need you to infiltrate their household, to pretend to be their friend. Once the child is born, you bring it here, with me."

"Uncle, don't be unreasonable. I can't kidnap a child."

"Of course you can." King Sterling crossed his arms over his chest. "You're a resourceful boy."

Winter shook his head resolutely. "Even if I did agree to it, such an act would defeat the entire purpose of me being there. You'd practically be signing up for war."

King Sterling waved a hand, dismissing his words. "Don't you worry about that. It's all under control. You just do what I say and obey orders."

The mere thought of separating a family for his uncle's pleasure made Winter sick to his stomach. "No," Winter said. "I will not."

His uncle got up and glowered at him. "Winter Tomacelli, as your king and by my authority and the power of my nation, I am ordering you to bring that child to me."

The words washed over Winter like a shower of ice water. Winter might be able to take some liberties with small things, but if he disobeyed his uncle, he could lose all privileges of his throne, and even his life. Sidhe legislation allowed for the king to execute traitors of the nation, and an outright "no" to an order like that could be qualified as an act of betrayal.

Was this the real reason of this unreasonable command? Did his uncle want him dead? It would make sense since there were many others healers out there that could easily deal with an injury inflicted by magic.

Winter considered his options and realized one thing. If he refused, he would not be helpful to anyone. His uncle would just recruit someone else and probably imprison Winter if he didn't feel comfortable with killing him.

"Very well," he replied, the words tasting bitter in his mouth. "It will be as you say, Your Majesty."

His uncle grinned at him. "Excellent. I knew you'd see things my way. You always were a smart boy."

Winter forced a smile, but in his mind, he was already imagining a plan. King Sterling had no idea just how smart Winter was. And no matter what happened, Winter would not allow Sterling to destroy the nation Winter's parents had died to protect.

Chapter One

The first time Corbin had seen the Alpha mansion on Soren Wade's pack lands, he'd noticed in surprise that it held more security than he'd ever seen in one place. That hadn't changed over the years. In fact, as Corbin walked through the gates of the mansion, he mentally noted that the building was surrounded by more people than usual.

Not that it surprised him. Recent events had made it necessary. And now, the situation had become worse with the unexpected involvement of the Sidhe.

Since he was well known here, he reached the front door without being stopped. Just as he readied himself to knock, the door opened and he found himself facing his brother.

"What do you mean, you brought a Sidhe in?" he asked without preamble. "It's the Sidhe that messed your life up in the first place."

Preston arched a brow. "And hello to you, too. It's nice to see you so well."

Corbin scowled at his brother. "Don't mess with me, Pres. Surely you realize how risky this is."

His brother nodded. "I know, but we don't have any choice." Preston opened and led Corbin inside. "The spells that were cast on our guards are only breakable by magic, the type that incubi don't have. We need their help."

That might be the case, but Corbin still wasn't happy about it. He couldn't get over the fact that his own mother had plotted with Elder Adele Mercier to curse Layton into falling in love with Corbin instead of his actual mate, Preston.

In a way, he was still puzzled about the whole thing. Neither she nor the elder Sidhe had ever admitted to how they had figured out Preston was Layton's mate in the first place. It bothered him, and it gave him the feeling that the Sidhe were one step ahead of him.

"I don't like it," he told his brother as they entered a receiving room.

Preston shrugged. "I haven't spent so much time with him since Layton is just as stingy as you about the whole thing. Honestly, I myself don't particularly like him. But he's quiet, and he hasn't given us any fuss."

Fussy or not, the man was still a Sidhe. Corbin took a deep breath. Perhaps it wasn't a good idea to judge an entire nation after only having contact with a couple of its people. After all, every species had its rotten apples. God only knew there were plenty among the shape-shifters as well. Corbin would give this new Sidhe a chance. The guy probably deserved that much if he was healing people who considered themselves his enemies.

"What's his name anyway?" he asked Preston.

"Winter Tomacelli," the other lynx replied. He checked the antique clock on the wall. "Come on. I'll take you to meet him. By now, he must be finished with his morning sessions."

Preston dragged Corbin out of the room and toward the adjacent backyard. The mansion didn't have an actual garden since it was surrounded by trees wherever the eye could see. But benches and tables had been placed in a clearing close by, and this recreation area was only separated from the main house by tall, ornate fences.

On one of the benches in question, Corbin saw a slender redhead, seemingly reading a book. There didn't seem to be anyone else around, so Corbin surmised that must be the Sidhe.

Winter looked up as Corbin and Preston approached. His gaze fixed on Corbin, and for a few moments, Corbin was lost in those beautiful orbs.

To Corbin's knowledge, most Sidhe were blond, but not Winter. Winter had long crimson hair, the color almost bloody. Coupled with his ice-blue eyes, he made for quite a striking sight. Corbin had honestly never seen anyone more beautiful. He snapped out of his trance when Preston started to introduce them. "Greetings, Winter. This is my brother, Corbin."

Winter offered him a small, neutral smile as he got up from the bench. "It's a pleasure. My name is Winter Tomacelli. I've heard a lot about you, Mr. Mckenna."

Normally, when Corbin spoke to a person he was attracted to, he'd pump up the flirtation. In a different situation, he might have said, "I'm sure they're all lies. Well, most of them." He could almost imagine the scene, with him being his usual charming self and the Sidhe melting in his arms.

But of course, he could not say or do such things. Winter was not a prospective fuck, at least not yet. If Corbin decided Winter truly meant them no ill, all bets were off.

For now, Corbin dusted off his diplomacy skills and went with a neutral reply. "So have I. My brother tells me you've been very helpful with healing our men."

Winter shrugged. "It was the least I could do. I can never begin to understand why Elder Mercier did what she did in the first place."

"On that point, we're agreed," Corbin answered. "I do have a question for you, if I may be so bold."

Winter looked startled. "Of course. If there's anything I can do to help."

"Have you made any progress in finding out who was behind my brother's situation? No one should have figured out Layton was Preston's mate except them."

"I can't answer that question, except with guesses. My best bet is that the warlocks somehow figured it out. They have scrying methods that go way beyond my power of comprehension. But I haven't been able to confirm these suspicions, I'm afraid, as the guilty parties have been released in exchange for peace."

"Do you believe that deal was a bad idea?" Preston inquired. "We did free Elder Mercier in your uncle's custody as well."

"I'm not questioning your decision," Winter shot back. "I'm just stating the facts. With the guilty parties gone, there is no way I could be able to tell you more."

"I see." Corbin interfered in the conversation before his brother could become even more incensed. Strikingly, even if when he'd first arrived here, he'd been just as intent to judge the Sidhe as untrustworthy, he wasn't so willing to do so now.

Something inside him just begged to reach out and touch Winter. He suppressed the urge, knowing that circumstances were far too complicated for him to indulge. He wasn't the one who'd been hurt most by the meddling fae, but his relationship with his brother had suffered greatly because of their interference. He was inclined to trust in Winter, but his instincts could have just been deceived by his unruly cock.

"Thank you for your answer," he told Winter formally. "I appreciate the insight. It's been weighing on my mind a lot."

"I'd be happy to help out with anything else you require," the Sidhe answered.

He was so lovely, and Corbin wondered if he would be just as obedient in bed. This time, Corbin couldn't control the maddening desire to touch the Sidhe. Leaning in closer, he brushed a lock of gorgeous red hair from Winter's face. "And I would be honored if you'd considered me a friend during your stay here."

The Sidhe broke away from his hold so quickly Corbin's head snapped back. "Thank you for the offer," Winter said with a tight smile. "You flatter me. But now I really must go. Please excuse me."

And with that, the Sidhe took off, leaving a bewildered and very enchanted Corbin behind. He watched Winter go without knowing whether to stare at that gorgeous ass or the sway of the beautiful red hair.

"What in the world, Corb?" Preston asked under his breath once Winter was gone. "You are not fucking that Sidhe."

"Not yet, I'm not," Corbin replied, turning toward Preston. When his brother just glared, Corbin squeezed the younger lynx's shoulder. "Relax. I know my priorities. I just have a feeling he's not so bad as you think."

"You weren't quite so insistent earlier," Preston noted. "I worry that this is just your cock speaking."

Corbin didn't grace that with a reply. Instead, he once again looked in the direction where Winter had disappeared. Perhaps he was allowing his libido to rule over his mind, but God, how could he help it?

* * * *

One year later

The huge courtyard of the Cunningham mansion was filled with people, some of them guests, others staff. Waiters swirled around, carrying trays with champagne glasses. There was so much hustle and bustle that Corbin's head was starting to hurt.

He'd retreated to a somewhat more secluded corner, trying to avoid the better part of the gathering. Usually, he could be found where the party was at its most intense, but not today.

Today, Corbin was in a strange mood. His friends, twins Morgan and Layton Cunningham, had officially registered their matings. Since they'd always been inseparable, they'd done it in the same ceremony. As such, their parents had thrown a huge party, inviting all their friends and acquaintances.

Corbin felt a little strange, mostly because it was his own brother who'd mated Layton Cunningham. For many years, Layton had romantically pursued Corbin, even if Corbin had never encouraged his advances. Oh, Layton was gorgeous, no doubt about it, and if Corbin wanted to be honest, he'd have fucked Layton a long time ago had he thought he could get away with it. Thankfully, he'd not pursued that impulse as it turned out Layton had actually been the mate of Corbin's little brother.

Seeing Preston sit together with Layton was quite humbling. It was true that Corbin's relationship with his brother had grown more distant throughout past years, but now, it really dawned on Corbin that he was no longer the most important thing in Preston's life. Then again, that had probably changed a long time ago, only Corbin hadn't wanted to admit it.

There were a lot of people around Corbin's brother lining up to see the new additions to the family, Morgan's son, Elian, and Layton's baby, Shea. Elian was quite good-natured about all the attention, something probably caused by his half-incubus nature. Apparently, incubi reveled in emotion, so it was only natural that Elian would enjoy being fussed over. Layton's son, however, seemed cranky, although that didn't make him any less lovable.

Of course, the proud parents were always looming over both boys, so there was no danger to either child. Corbin wished he could be closer to them and hold his tiny nephew in his arms, but sadly, he felt like he would choke if another woman he'd slept with in the past tried to flirt with him. They intercepted him wherever he went, and the last thing Corbin wanted was to draw attention to himself when this was supposed to be Preston's special day. Well, there was a little more to it than that, mostly because of a certain person Corbin didn't know what to think or feel about. But now was not the time or the place to worry about such confusing emotions.

"Hey, what are you doing here all by your lonesome?" a male voice suddenly asked.

Corbin turned to see his friend, Isaac, approach. He grinned at the other man. Isaac was usually somewhat more reclusive, so it was no surprise that he had tried to find refuge from the crowd as well. "Just taking a break," he said. "I want to wait until all the fuss dies down and go see Shea."

"I went to him just earlier," he said. "He's a beautiful baby."

Warm pleasure coursed through him as if the child was his, not Preston's. It almost didn't matter because he already loved Shea and was very protective and proud of the beautiful boy. "Thanks," he told Isaac. "What about you? What are you up to?"

Isaac shrugged. "Just barely managed to escape Mother's clutches. Since one son is happy, she wants the other one to find a mate, too."

Corbin snickered. "Carson's twenty years older than you. Of course he has a mate."

"And children older than me," Isaac said in a mock-mournful tone. It was a private joke of theirs that Angel and Clark, Carson's adoptive sons, were older than Isaac, their uncle.

"I don't envy your family tree," Corbin said. Sometimes, it gave him a headache just to think about how Isaac was half brother with both Carson and Carson's mate, Brody. His third half brother, Soren, also had three children, which left Isaac an uncle to five people older than him.

"Stop smirking." Isaac hit his shoulder playfully. His expression sobered. "Seriously, though, are you okay? Sulking in the corner is usually my domain."

"I'm fine," Corbin replied automatically. "The idea of having a mated younger brother just takes some getting used to."

"I suppose," Isaac mused. "Anyway, if you're not up to celebrating, mind if I stick around here with you?"

"Of course I don't mind." Corbin chuckled. "At least you and I will get to catch up a bit."

"I'm afraid I haven't done anything interesting lately." Isaac sighed. "You know, just when I finally managed to be accepted at the university, everyone's leaving and finding mates. It seems like I'm always one step behind."

This time, the words were spoken in a serious tone, and honestly, Corbin felt for the man. Isaac had always gotten the short end of the stick since he was the first and only known hybrid between a lamb and a wolf. To this day, Corbin had no idea how his friend's shifting abilities worked. Not to mention that for a long time, Isaac's father, elder werewolf Kevin Wade, had been very protective of his youngest son, for reasons still unknown. That protectiveness had isolated Isaac, and even if Corbin and his family and friends always tried to include Isaac in their activities, sometimes, things didn't work out the way they planned.

"You're very young still," he told Isaac. "Don't be in a hurry to grow up. Live a little. At your age, I was sleeping with every female shifter that crossed my path." And some male, but those he hadn't mentioned to his family due to the Layton situation.

To his surprise, Isaac snickered. "Do you have any idea how old that makes you sound?" Isaac pretended to imitate an old man, "Oh, these young'uns. I remember the good old days, when—"

Corbin reached for Isaac, interrupting the joking remark. "You're a brat, you know that?" he asked when the other man dodged him, laughing.

"I guess I am," Isaac replied, snickering. Still, he seemed in a better mood, so Corbin's job was done.

All of a sudden, the feel of an approaching presence drew Corbin's attention. He turned to scan the crowd, his heart already starting to race.

"Hey, look who's here." Isaac pointed toward a slender man who was making his way through the crowd. "Our own resident Sidhe."

Corbin's body immediately responded just at the sight of the beautiful magic user. Winter had been his obsession since the first day Corbin had seen the Sidhe. Corbin had tried everything, every seduction technique tested on both male and females, but his attempts to draw Winter's attention had always been met with cool disdain. The failure disheartened Corbin, but he refused to give up. He wanted to bury his hands in the silken mass of red hair and touch the creamy skin that just begged to kissed. Since the day they'd met, Winter had never given him the chance to enjoy its softness. He wanted to unveil the treasures of Winter's body and make love to the Sidhe until neither of them could stand.

But Winter always refused him, even if Corbin could have sworn that sometimes, the Sidhe wanted to yield. Corbin took a deep breath to steel himself. He had another chance today. Didn't everyone say that weddings were the best place to get laid? Maybe the joyfulness of the day would have mellowed Winter's temper a little.

"Excuse me," he told Isaac. "I believe I'm needed elsewhere."

Isaac laughed, but not in a mocking way. "Good luck, my friend. I think you're going to need it."

Corbin agreed with Isaac's assessment, but he didn't let it change his mind. He started to navigate through the hustle and bustle, ignoring the occasional sounds of people calling his name.

Winter was with the group hovering around the children, something that didn't surprise Corbin in the slightest. The Sidhe seemed to be one of the few people—other than family—to which Shea showed pure affection.

He reached the group just as Layton was handing his son to Winter so that the Sidhe could greet Shea. "Hey, brother," Preston said. "Where did you run off to?"

"Just taking a break," Corbin replied with a grin. "After all, it wouldn't do for the party to be focused on me and not on you."

Layton snorted but didn't say anything, used to the exchanges between Corbin and Preston. All the while, Corbin didn't take his gaze off Winter for a single moment. The Sidhe looked so beautiful with Shea in his arms. Corbin couldn't help but imagine Winter holding another child, Corbin's son or daughter. And God, where the hell had that thought come from? Corbin lusted for Winter, sure, but from that to children...No way. Besides, the fact that Corbin's brother had married a male who could give birth didn't mean that was the norm.

But as much as Corbin struggled to remain reasonable, it was very hard to do so when he heard Winter whisper Sidhe endearments to Shea. It was just too adorable, and it made Corbin's heart ache for something he didn't dare identify.

And then Winter looked up at him. For a few moments, their gazes met and locked. Corbin thought he saw a strange yearning in Winter's ice-blue eyes, but the fleeting impression vanished. "Greetings, Mr. Mckenna," the Sidhe said formally. "I believe you wanted to see your nephew?"

Corbin gave Preston and Layton a small look, asking for permission to take the child from Winter. When Layton nodded, Winter handed little Shea to Corbin. "Hey there, little guy," Corbin greeted his nephew, wiggling his fingers at the tiny child. He should have felt like an idiot, but he didn't.

His only reply was an adorable coo, but Shea did reach for his finger, like Corbin knew he would. His little hand took hold of Corbin's digit, barely managing to encompass it. It was like a secret handshake Corbin had discovered, and it felt so special. He wondered if his sudden desire to have a family with Winter was simply caused by his affection toward Shea. That made sense, in a way, although Corbin wasn't particularly happy with the explanation.

"Well, isn't this just precious?" A female voice suddenly sounded behind them.

Corbin turned, only to see Annabelle Wade approach, her husband in tow. Somewhere along the way, she'd picked up both her sons. Isaac looked pained while Carson just seemed amused.

"You look great with your nephew in your arms. When can we expect you to take a mate?"

Elder Wade arched a brow. "I have several females in the pack with broken hearts."

Corbin laughed. "I'm not the important one right now," he said.

On cue, Shea released a noise that Corbin identified as one of irritation. "I think someone needs his nap," Layton said as he took Shea from Corbin. "If you'll excuse me, I'll go take him to his room."

Everyone said good-bye to Shea and his birth father. Layton and Preston exchanged a brief kiss. As Layton began to walk away, Preston gave his mate a look of longing.

"Go on," Corbin told his brother. "Go with him. You know you want to."

"I can't just leave the guests," Preston protested.

"Nonsense," Annabelle said. "We're not just guests, we're family. And besides, many of us understand what it's like to be recently mated."

Annabelle Wade was a ewe-shifter who'd once belonged to the Ramston flock. She had met Elder Kevin Wade after her son, Carson, had mated his, and the rest was history. Theirs had been a whirlwind romance that had intrigued many people and scandalized even more. But the elder hadn't cared, and Corbin didn't blame the man. She was a real lady, and if she'd been a wolf, she'd have made for a great Alpha bitch. Hell, Corbin might not know much about current werewolf dynamics, but he thought that she had already taken up the duties of the regular Alpha female, in spite of being a ewe.

It was therefore not surprising that she understood Preston and had given him an out. Preston thanked her and rushed after his mate. There was no doubt that after the two happy parents dealt to the needs of their son, they'd probably satisfy some desires of their own.

"They're great together," Elder Wade commented, his gaze on his son. Isaac studiously ignored his father, which both amused and bothered Corbin. The werewolf shouldn't push his son so much if Isaac wasn't ready to take a mate. He already had four wonderful grandsons and a granddaughter, so he should be in no rush.

Either way, Corbin couldn't get involved. As close as the Mckennas were with the Wades, the elder werewolf would not allow outside interference in his family business. Besides, Corbin had his own problems to worry about, namely how to reach out to Winter.

As if guessing Corbin's thoughts, Winter suddenly said, "I should probably go, too."

"No, stay," Corbin blurted out. "I wanted to talk to you about something."

It wasn't exactly the smoothest come-on line Corbin had come up with, but it at least stopped Winter from leaving. He was frowning, but he hadn't left.

"Well, would you look at that?" Annabelle commented. "We haven't gone to see Elian. Come along," she said to her family. "I'm sure Corbin has better things to do than to sit here chatting with us."

Elder Wade took her hand, and together with Isaac and Carson, the couple started to walk away, leaving Corbin alone with Winter— or as alone as he could be in the middle of such a huge party.

"You wanted to talk to me?" Winter asked, his voice nearly inaudible.

Corbin couldn't believe how uncomfortable and out of depth he felt. Usually, he had no trouble in using his natural good looks to convince others to date him. Around Winter, he turned into a bumbling idiot.

"Yes," he answered, "but not here. Could we maybe have a small chat in private?"

Winter's frown deepened. "I don't think that would be a very good idea."

Corbin grabbed the Sidhe's arm before the other man could make his escape. "Please, Winter. Five minutes. Just five minutes of your time."

If anyone had told him a year back that one day, he'd find himself in this situation, Corbin wouldn't have believed it. He'd never had to plead for attention from a prospective romantic interest, but now, he'd do that and more if it got Winter to pay attention to him.

"All right," Winter said, his expression only showing reluctance. "Five minutes."

Corbin led Winter away from the party, deciding he could sneak out briefly now that his brother and nephew were gone. He led Winter inside and found the first vacant room, a sort of receiving lounge where Skylar Cunningham usually entertained guests. Since the party had spilled over into the courtyard and gardens, it was empty now.

As Winter obediently walked inside, Corbin struggled to find the right thing to say. Okay, so he'd gotten Winter's attention. But he had five minutes to make sure his luck held.

"All right, Mr. Mckenna, I'm listening," Winter prodded.

Corbin grimaced at the formality of the address. "Please, call me Corbin. We've known each other for a year now."

Winter released a sigh. "Fine. Corbin. Was that what you wanted, or do you need something else?"

The sound of his name on Winter's lips made goose bumps flourish over Corbin's skin. He managed to keep himself in check, just barely. "Actually, I wanted to ask you if you'd like to go out to dinner with me. Maybe see a movie or go on a walk. Whatever you like."

Lame. Double lame. God, could he really not come up with something better than that?

The Sidhe arched a brow. "You mean, like a date?"

The skepticism in Winter's voice didn't bode well. "Yes, like a date," Corbin answered. "Is that so hard to believe?"

Winter just gave him a bemused look. "No. I suppose I just didn't expect it."

"Why not?" Corbin took one step closer. He might as well make things clear. He didn't have anything to lose. "You must know how I feel about you."

The Sidhe shook his head. "I know you want to get into my pants, but beyond that, there has been no talk of feelings."

With Winter right there, Corbin couldn't resist encroaching on the Sidhe's personal space. Winter's expression shifted, becoming a bit apprehensive. He fidgeted, his gaze straying, as if unable to look straight at Corbin. Beyond that obviously uncomfortable façade, Corbin's beast detected something more. He sensed arousal. Winter wasn't as immune to Corbin as he wanted to seem.

With every step that Corbin took, Winter tried to back off, until at last, there was no place left to go. Corbin crowded the Sidhe against the wall and pressed his body against Winter's slender one. He inhaled deeply, Winter's scent the most potent aphrodisiac he could have ever discovered.

"Why are you running from me?" he murmured in the other man's ear. "There's something between us. I know you can feel it, too."

He indulged in fulfilling his longtime desire of burying his fingers in Winter's crimson locks and felt a shudder course through the beautiful Sidhe. They were close, so very close now. Corbin only had to lean a few inches farther and his lips would be on Winter's.

Even knowing how foolish it was to do this, Corbin couldn't resist. He pressed his mouth to Winter's, at last tasting the man he'd desired for so long. At first, Winter melted against him, moaning as he parted his lips to allow Corbin entrance. The hard bulge of Winter's cock nudged against Corbin's thigh, notifying him just how the Sidhe felt about Corbin.

Corbin wanted to take Winter in his arms and peel off the layers of clothing that separated their bodies. He yearned to be inside Winter, to claim the Sidhe as his. Winter would be tight and hot like a velvet fist, Corbin just knew it. And God, just the anticipation drove Corbin to the brink of climax.

He was so lost in his lust-induced trance that when Winter suddenly pushed him away, the reason didn't immediately register. The loss of the heat and Winter's delicious scent seemed so much more important. But as he looked into Winter's eyes, he understood he'd made a grave mistake.

"I'm sorry," Winter said, his voice weak but once again holding its usual chill. "We do have chemistry, I will grant you that. But this is not a good time for me to engage in a sexual liaison. Please, don't approach me again with such a proposition."

With a speed that surprised Corbin, Winter brushed past him and practically ran out of the room. Corbin blinked in shock before cursing himself for pushing Winter too hard, too fast. Clearly, Winter was reluctant to attempt a relationship, and Corbin's reputation of a Casanova probably didn't help. Corbin took a deep breath and focused on taming his raging libido. He would have to find a different way to reach out to the Sidhe because the alternative was unacceptable.

Chapter Two

Winter fled as quickly as he could, heading toward the room he'd been given in the Cunningham mansion. It was a guest room that had quickly become his, just like the shape-shifters here had started to become his family.

But the emotions Corbin Mckenna roused in him were anything but familial. The lynx-shifter made Winter question everything he'd come here to do. A strange yearning filled Winter every time he saw Corbin, and the fact that he knew Corbin wanted him, too, didn't help.

Winter ran faster, hoping against all hope that he could escape his own doubts and guilt. It was not to be, as just as he went up the staircase, he ran into Alexis Whitaker, no, Alexis Cunningham.

In spite of the resentfulness between their two peoples, Alexis had been among the first to befriend Winter. Winter had helped heal Alexis's brother from a spell that had threatened to leave him catatonic, but his presence had still been viewed with much suspicion. However, in spite of Winter being a complete outsider, the incubus had supported him and encouraged him when Winter had been down.

"Hey, there," Alexis said. "What's wrong, Winter?"

It wasn't surprising that Alexis had sensed the situation. Incubi had the power to see into other individuals' emotions. Even so, he felt uncomfortable to actually reveal the true extent of his problem.

"Nothing," he lied.

Alexis arched a brow. "You expect me to believe that? Don't be ridiculous. Is it Corbin?"

Winter gaped at the demon, shocked even if he should have expected Alexis to know about the whole thing.

"Don't look at me like that." Alexis laughed. "I don't have to be an incubus to see you two are really into each other. What did he do now?"

"Nothing," Winter said again. When Alexis crossed his arms over his chest and tapped his foot impatiently, Winter relented and decided to add, "He asked me out on a date."

"Well, that's a good thing," Alexis said. "Why are you running like you have an army of tin men on your heels?"

Winter offered Alexis a weak smile at the reference of the Sidhe's weakness to iron. It should have bothered him, but for him, it meant just one more hint that his fae nature was accepted. His smile died when he recalled Alexis was waiting for an answer. "I'm really not ready for a relationship right now," he said.

Alexis released a thoughtful hum. "Well, you know your heart best, but if you'll allow me, I'll give you a friendly piece of advice. Corbin is a good man. He might have slept around a lot in the past, but he cares about you, more than he himself would like to admit. Don't let a good thing go to waste because you're afraid."

A burst of anger assaulted Winter. What did Alexis know? Yes, Winter was afraid, and for good reason. What would Corbin say if he found out the real motivation behind Winter's extended stay with the Cunninghams? What would Alexis himself think? Winter could only imagine how Layton and Preston would look at him, especially with the trust the couple had shown him. Yes, he had many fears, but in the circumstances, weren't they justified?

Winter knew that he'd soon have to tell his hosts the truth. He could no longer hold his uncle in check. He'd stalled for as long as he could. When that happened, when he at last revealed his purpose here, everyone would hate him. Winter didn't think he could stand it if he accepted Corbin's affection, only to have it turn into hate later on.

"I don't mean to overstep my boundaries," Alexis said, obviously sensing his emotions. "I merely want you and Corbin to be happy. I made a lot of mistakes that nearly cost me my life, and Elian's. I don't want that sort of thing to happen to anyone else."

The gentle tone of the incubus's voice made Winter's anger deflate. "I know. Thanks. I just…I'll think about it, all right?"

"You do that." Alexis hugged him briefly. "Now, I believe my son needs me. Half incubus he might be, but he still needs his rest from all the agitation."

And with that, Alexis waved good-bye and took his leave. Winter watched him go in a mix of shock and confusion. Had the incubus only come around here because he'd sensed Winter's distress? If so, it made Winter's secret keeping even more treasonous.

His heart heavy, Winter made his way to his room. As soon as he closed the door behind him, he felt both safer and lonelier. He imagined Corbin, the way the sunlight would catch in the lynx's blond hair and how his blue eyes twinkled when he smiled. Oh, how he wanted to take a leap of faith, to accept what Corbin offered. But he couldn't. His life didn't allow for love right now, and Winter had never been one for no-strings sex.

Winter sighed and plopped facedown on his bed. He was so very tired. It seems like he hadn't slept in weeks. During Layton's pregnancy, it had been easy enough to thwart his uncle's questions, but now, Sterling was demanding action. He wanted Shea, and he was willing to do whatever it took for it.

As such, Winter was forced to come up with more and more excuses, all the while watching over Shea just in case his uncle saw through his lies. He couldn't do it for much longer. He needed a plan, a real plan beyond stalling. He had to approach Byron Cunningham. The shark-shifter had to know his grandson was in peril. Besides, Byron was one of the most capable men Winter knew. He'd certainly know what to do. Winter might have thought he could deal with his uncle alone, but it had been folly from the very beginning.

As if summoned by his thoughts, a trickle of magic niggled at Winter's consciousness. Winter lifted his head, only to see a white, glowing sphere manifest out of the nothingness.

Dread assaulted him. He already knew who the magical message was from. His uncle had contacted him many times in the same way. In this house, the only people who could detect it were the incubi, and while the Whitaker family was powerful, they specialized in emotions, not cloak-and-dagger magical messaging.

Knowing that delaying the inevitable would only make things worse, Winter left the bed and went to the sphere. Slowly, he touched it, feeling the familiar hint of his uncle's magic within. It was strange, really. He'd always thought he'd be able to feel evil in someone's spiritual energy. Elder Mercier, for example, had always given him a bad feeling. But with his uncle, it never seemed like the man had dark magic. Perhaps Sterling had managed to cloak his wickedness somehow. Because no doubt about it, a man capable of separating a child from his family could be nothing but wicked.

The sphere identified Winter's own magic and an image appeared in front of Winter, King Sterling's image. He was dressed in full regalia, as if to emphasize his position, and the cold look on his face didn't bode well for Winter's future. "Greetings, Winter. I will be brief. Your recent message displeased me greatly. Your lack of obeisance is both disappointing and bothersome. It would behoove you to cease this behavior at once, or I will be forced to take measures that will cause us both great distress. I do not want to brand you a traitor, Winter. Bring me that child, and I will forget about your rebellion. You have two days."

The image dimmed until it disappeared entirely. Winter's mind worked furiously, trying to find a way out of a situation that seemed inescapable. If he obeyed his uncle, he went against his every value. If he disobeyed, he would most likely lose all rights to the throne, surrendering full control of the nation into Sterling's hands. Surely there had to be someone he could turn to, someone who would see

how unfair this situation was. In fact, Winter shouldn't have to be his
uncle's errand boy. He was a prince, and he had power and respect in
his own right.

But the Sidhe were a conservative people. They would not
understand Winter's choice and most likely would see things the way
Sterling wanted to paint them. Winter had hoped that, once he came
into his thirtieth year and could legally take over the throne, he'd be
able to encourage some openness between shifters and Sidhe. But of
course, Sterling was unlikely to let go of the crown so easily, and in
the current circumstances, it was doubtful that Winter would even be
able to keep his title.

An earlier picture flashed through Winter's mind's eye, that of
Corbin holding Shea in his arms. And then that awkward invitation to
go on a date from the lynx. It had been so sweet, and Winter had been
so very tempted to accept.

Whatever happened, he couldn't betray the people who'd opened
their hearts to him. He couldn't betray Corbin, who already meant so
much to him, as much as Winter tried to deny it. But would this
decision mean he was letting down his own people, the same ones
Winter's parents had led for so many years?

Shaking himself, Winter decided questions would not solve a
thing. One thing was certain. He needed to approach his hosts and tell
them about King Sterling's plan. He'd have to wait until the mating
celebration was over, though. The last thing he wanted was to spoil
such a special day.

Winter considered going out and mingling with the crowd again
but quickly decided against it. He didn't think he could put up a
façade of cool calm when he was crumbling inside. Instead, he lay
back on the bed, trying to think about anything else that wasn't the
horrid situation he found himself in.

Inevitably, his mind drifted to Corbin, to the lynx's gorgeous,
hard-muscled body and his handsome face. Winter knew he shouldn't
indulge in this, but he couldn't help it. The arousal that had been

dimmed by his nervousness and apprehension returned with a vengeance.

His cock strained against the zipper of his pants, and Winter reached down to release his prick.

A gasp escaped him as he took his hard shaft into his hand. He closed his eyes, imagining it was Corbin's fist massaging him, Corbin pleasuring him, caressing him like no one else had. Needing more, Winter kicked off his shoes and shimmied out of his pants and underwear. Now naked from the waist down, he reached behind himself, rubbing his fingers against his needy hole. He'd never had anyone invade him there. He'd wanted to save himself for The One, that special person who could touch his heart, not only his body.

But God help him, he wanted Corbin to be that person. He slipped the tip of one digit slowly inside, just a little bit, not daring to do more. The promise in his own touch made him whimper in delight. He wished he'd thought of getting some lubricant beforehand, but it was too late now. Besides, the slight burn caused by the invasion just added to the sensation.

Pre-cum flowed liberally from the tip of his cock now as he imagined Corbin's hands on him. Courtesy of his Sidhe ancestry, Winter's own palms were softer, too soft. He squeezed his prick harder, hoping the pressure would compensate for the lack.

In his mind, it was Corbin's fingers up his ass and Corbin fisting his cock. Winter's hole ached with the need for a harder, deeper invasion, and his cock throbbed with the need to come. Winter allowed himself to fall completely in the heaven of his own imagination. He distantly heard his own voice crying out Corbin's name, but he couldn't bring himself to care.

How would Corbin be like when they made love? Would he be rough and make Winter feel his fucking or gentle, reaching out to Winter's heart? Just the question drove Winter closer to climax. He could almost see it now, the passion in Corbin's gaze, the way his body had felt against Winter's when they'd kissed, his hard cock insistently demanding attention. It had been the hardest thing Winter had done in his life to run away and not sink onto his knees to take Corbin's cock in his mouth.

Corbin would taste just heavenly, Winter knew it. His girth would be such that he'd make Winter's jaw hurt as he took Corbin's prick in his mouth. He would gag, but he'd love every moment of it. And then, after he'd pleasured Corbin with his mouth, the lynx would thrust that fat cock inside Winter's ass.

The sinful images Winter's mind conjured were too much to bear. Writhing at his own touch, he cried one more time before he spent his seed all over his hand. He lay there, panting, lost, and dazed, almost thinking that if he just opened his eyes, Corbin would be next to him on the bed, anticipating their next union.

But of course, that wasn't the case. As Winter's vision cleared, he found himself alone in his room and feeling emptier than ever. His little jack-off session hadn't solved a thing. If anything, it had brought even more contradicting emotions and questions.

Heaving a sigh, Winter left the bed and made his way to the bathroom. He wiped himself down, clearing the evidence of his forbidden desire from his skin. He'd just managed to clean up when he sensed a familiar presence nearby. At first, he thought he hadn't recovered from his fantasy, but then a knock sounded at the door of his room, confirming the initial impression. *Oh, God.* What could Corbin be doing here?

Winter hastily left the bathroom and started to dress. "Yes?" he called out as he did so.

"It's me," Corbin said from outside. "Corbin Mckenna," he added, as if Winter wouldn't know his voice and energy from those belonging to a million other people. "Could I maybe talk to you for a minute?"

"You already had five," Winter answered with far more snappishness than he'd have liked. Still, knowing that it was unlikely that Corbin would go, he pulled on his underwear and pants and tried to arrange the wild mass of his hair.

"I know, but I kind of wasted them." A deep sigh. "If you don't want to see me, I understand. I'll just talk from here."

Winter was horrified at the concept. He couldn't imagine making Corbin wait in front of his door like that. It just seemed wrong. Besides, most of the house inhabitants might be busy with the party downstairs, but anyone could come overhear. Winter was a private person, and he preferred it if he kept such intimacies behind closed doors. He guessed a part of him was as conservative as other Sidhe, after all.

With a sigh, Winter resigned himself to the inevitable. "You don't need to do that," he said.

He went to open the door, almost changing his mind when he saw the lynx standing in the doorway. Merely looking at Corbin reminded Winter of what he'd just done earlier. Heat flooded his face, and he once again cursed his redheaded nature. Why couldn't he have the luck of most of his acquaintances, who, in spite of their fair complexion, rarely blushed?

Forcing himself to muster a modicum of calm, he asked, "What is it now?"

"I merely wanted to apologize for earlier," Corbin replied. "I pushed too hard, even knowing that you weren't willing to start something with me." He paused, as if struggling for words. "So, I'd like to ask you one thing. If you don't want me as your lover, would you consider at least having me as a friend?"

Winter's eyes widened. He'd have expected anything but that. "Really?"

It was hypocritical of him to want platonic friendship from a man whose image he'd just jacked off to. Even so, it meant a lot to him that Corbin was willing to respect his decision and offer simple affection in spite of the way Winter had treated him.

Corbin nodded. "I know you find it hard to believe, but I…" Corbin took a deep breath, as if steeling himself for something. "I really do care about you. A lot."

Winter wanted to cry. How could he resist Corbin when with each second that passed, the lynx gave him more reasons to throw caution to the wind? More importantly, how would Winter bear it when Corbin hated him? After all, Winter was a traitor. He didn't deserve to receive such affection, and having it, only to lose it later, would be akin to hell.

"What is it, sweetheart?" Corbin asked, obviously sensing his distress. Was it Winter's imagination, or did Corbin start sniffing the air? His expression was strange, torn between dismay and anger. "Is someone in here? Did they hurt you?"

Winter blinked in surprise at the sudden change in topic. "Hurt me?" he repeated. "No. I…Who?"

Corbin seemed angry and confused now. "I just…I'm sorry. It's none of my business." He clenched his fists, as if trying to control his temper. "I should go. I didn't mean to interrupt."

In that moment, Winter understood. Shifters had very acute senses. Even if Winter had cleaned up, Corbin must have smelled sex on him.

He wanted to die. Obviously, Corbin thought Winter had been fucking someone else. His first guess had been that another guy had been forcing himself on Winter, which spoke volumes of Corbin's opinion of him. But when Winter had denied this…Well, it was clear that opinion had changed.

Winter had two options. He could let Corbin think he was a whore and a cock tease, or he could own up to his actions and tell Corbin the truth. There was no real choice between the two, was there?

* * * *

Idiot. Corbin was such an idiot. He'd been convinced Winter was an innocent, and probably had his own more serious reason why he'd decided to refuse Corbin's advances. He'd been over their every exchange in his head and decided that he could wait for a while and give Winter time. He'd even figured that if he couldn't be Winter's lover, he could at least be the Sidhe's friend.

God, how ridiculous he must have seemed to the Sidhe. The great Casanova, reduced to a pleading mess, all because of a Sidhe who'd led him around by his dick. And the worst thing was that he didn't know which emotion humiliated him more, the anger or the hurt. *Hurt.* On top of his ridiculous proposition, he had to suffer from heartbreak, too. *Christ.*

He had to cut his losses and flee to his room, where he could lick his wounds in private. He didn't think he could face the party now, especially not knowing which guest had replaced him in Winter's bed. That was the strangest thing. Even if the scent of sex was crystal clear, he couldn't smell anyone else except Winter around. Perhaps it was for the best. As furious as he was, he was liable to kill the person who'd dared to touch Winter, and that would ruin Preston's special day.

So, instead, he did his best to keep a straight face and said, "I'll leave you to what you were doing. Just…ignore what I told you."

As he started to turn, however, a small hand caught his wrist. "Please don't go." Winter's voice was nearly a whisper. "It's not what you think."

Winter's touch distracted Corbin like crazy, so he freed himself from the Sidhe's grip. "And what would you know of what I think?" he bit out, unable to control the anger in his tone.

Truly, he had no right to be jealous or even pissed at Winter. The Sidhe had never confessed to any interest in a relationship with Corbin. He'd admitted they had chemistry, but that didn't mean anything. It had all been Corbin's stupid suppositions. For all he knew, Winter had a lover all this time and had been reluctant to tell everyone.

For that reason, he felt guilty when Winter winced. No, he shouldn't blame Winter for his own mistakes. Honestly, Corbin couldn't believe Winter had deliberately deceived him, so it was unfair to spout his fury at the young Sidhe.

With a sigh, he took Winter's hand and kissed it. "I'm sorry. I shouldn't have shouted. I respect your choice."

If anything, his words seemed to make Winter even more reasonable. Something was seriously wrong here. In spite of his earlier anger and the knowledge that Winter didn't belong to him, protectiveness swelled in his heart. If Winter did have a lover, it seemed the other guy wasn't treating the sweet Sidhe right.

"I know I don't have any right to ask you this," Winter murmured, "but I really do need a friend. If you'd just hear me out for a minute, I'd be very thankful."

Corbin nodded, unable to refuse Winter anything. The Sidhe looked somewhat relieved and offered him a tremulous smile. "Come in, please."

The poor fae seemed so afraid that Corbin's every instinct begged to soothe him. This need to protect was something he hadn't experienced before, at least not to this extent. Even with his young nephew, the urge to shield him from all harm wasn't this intense. He had to keep a cool head and take whatever Winter had to tell him in stride.

Winter's quarters were just like any other of the guest rooms. Even with all the time he'd been here, Winter hadn't changed a thing. Still, the feel of him, his scent and his warmth were all over the place. Corbin wanted to climb into Winter's bed and roll around in the Sidhe's sheets, to inhale's Winter's scent so deeply he'd never forget it.

Instead, he focused on the fae's earnest face. "What is it, sweetheart?" The endearment slipped out naturally without Corbin being able to hold it back. "What's wrong?"

"Let me just begin by saying that there was never anyone here." He was blushing fiercely, Corbin realized. "You left me in quite a predicament, and I had to err...take matters into my own hands. Literally."

Corbin's mind short-circuited at the picture those words conjured. Winter touching himself, masturbating, perhaps to images of Corbin, made Corbin's knees go weak and his body respond.

"You really didn't need to do that," he said huskily. "I'd have gladly helped you out."

Winter took a deep breath and looked away. "I know. But I had my reasons why I said no. Everyone here, and you in particular, mean the world to me. But I'm afraid I have deceived you."

"Deceived us?" Corbin repeated. "You don't have a deceitful bone in your body."

As he spoke the words, Corbin realized he believed them, too, and yet he'd automatically jumped to the conclusion that Winter had slept with someone else and made fun of him behind his back. He shook off the bitter taste of the guilt and decided he'd never again allow himself to fall prey to jealousy so easily.

On his side, Winter seemed increasingly miserable. "I wish that were true," he answered. "You know how I told everyone that I'm the nephew of the current Sidhe king?" When Corbin nodded, Winter continued, "That's true, but I'm also a prince and the true heir of the former king. My father and mother were killed in an Unseelie attack, and I was too young to deal with the problems of a nation in turmoil. For that reason, my uncle took over. I am under his authority, at least until I reach my thirtieth year and can make an active bid for the throne."

Corbin had known Winter was royalty, but the idea that the Sidhe might actually be the leader of a nation was mind-boggling.

Compared to that, Corbin had very little achievements. While he'd done some work for his father when the other lynx had needed it, he actually loved running his auto shop. Once upon a time, he'd been a partier, but now he preferred leading a quiet life. How could that sort of thing possibly measure up to the glamour of Winter's existence?

But that wasn't the point here, now was it? Corbin couldn't believe that such a simple omission had caused so much torment for the young fae. "I'm sure you'll be a great king," he offered. "But there's more to it than that, isn't there?"

Winter nodded. "A year back, when the Cunninghams visited my uncle, he told me that he wanted me to come here to help heal those injured. He also instructed me that once Layton's baby was born, I should steal the child and bring him to the Sidhe palace."

Nothing could have surprised Corbin more than such an admission. He knew King Sterling had demanded Shea in exchange for a peace treaty between the Sidhe and the shifters, but he'd never expected Winter to be in on it.

If it had been anyone else telling him this, Corbin would have made sure the person in question never saw Shea, or anyone from his family, ever again. But this was Winter, and as biased as Corbin's judgment of the Sidhe might be, he knew Winter would never wish Shea ill. It was quite obvious that Winter did not approve of his uncle's methods. Judging by Winter's defeated stance, the Sidhe also expected to be rejected for this secret.

Corbin's heart hurt for Winter's pain. The beautiful fae had obviously been carrying this burden alone for far too long. "He forced you into it somehow," Corbin said. "What did he threaten you with?"

Winter's eyes widened. "I…You…You don't hate me?"

"I could never hate you," Corbin answered. "Now tell me everything."

Still looking a bit awed, Winter started to explain. By the time the Sidhe had finished, Corbin was so angry he couldn't see straight. How could King Sterling do such a thing to Winter? How could Winter be forced to choose between his people and the shifters he'd come to care about?

Corbin would not allow Winter to suffer anymore. "You're not alone in this," he told the Sidhe. "The Cunninghams have to be told, but I'll be there with you every step of the way."

The relief on Winter's face was staggering. The Sidhe actually seemed close to tears. "Thank you. I don't think I can face them on my own." He wiped his eyes, confirming Corbin's guess about his near crying. "I should talk to them as soon as possible. Would you come with me?"

"Of course." Corbin kissed Winter's forehead. "I'll wait for you outside while you change."

Winter released a small laugh. "Right. I wouldn't want Byron to scent me like you did."

It was probably pointless to tell Winter that Byron would most likely smell him anyway. The shark's abilities awed and scared Corbin a little. But there was no reason to make Winter even more nervous than he already was.

As he'd said he would, Corbin left the room and closed the door behind himself. He leaned against the wall, musing about what he'd learned. He had to think coolly about this and separate his reason from the anger. Why would the Sidhe king be so adamant on having Shea? Shea was only a shifter baby, granted, a lovely one, but still, one without any magical abilities whatsoever. What would Sterling have to gain from kidnapping him? Was it only a ploy to steal the throne from Winter?

He was still musing over these questions when the door opened and Winter came out. He offered Corbin a small smile and said, "Okay. I'm ready."

Corbin took Winter's hand, marveling at how right it felt to hold it in his own larger one. He thought that maybe Winter felt the same because the Sidhe seemed to relax a little. "Thank you for this,

Corbin," he said. "I don't know what will happen, but it doesn't seem so hopeless anymore."

"No problem, sweetheart. Now let's go find the Cunninghams."

As they walked, Corbin mused over these new revelations. In his heart, a new certainty was rising. There was only one answer behind this yearning, this feeling of rightness. Winter was his mate. Corbin had been so blind and refused to see it in fear of what it would mean for his old life. But now, he realized his foolishness. As soon as he could, he would approach Winter with his heart open and he'd confess his feelings. Perhaps it was corny and lame, but as long as Corbin had Winter, he could deal with being called a hopeless romantic.

Chapter Three

The party was still in full swing when Corbin led Winter into the gardens. As expected, Skylar Cunningham busied himself with making everyone feel right at home. Byron was nowhere to be seen, and Winter surmised the shark-shifter must have taken refuge somewhere. The man was not at all a social butterfly like his mate, although, to his credit, he did make the attempt.

In a way, Winter wished he could talk to Byron first. Skylar had been great during Winter's entire stay here, and he was fiercely protective of his children. Winter would much rather face Byron's wrath than Skylar's disdain and disappointment.

In the end, Skylar intercepted them before Winter could be ready to face the seahorse. "Hello, Winter. Is everything all right? I saw Alexis earlier, and he told me you seemed upset."

Most likely, Skylar had drawn it out of the incubus because the seahorse had a way of making a person open up to him. Taking a deep breath, Winter said, "Actually, I'd like to talk to you and your mate, if it's possible."

Skylar arched a brow. "Is it urgent, or can it wait until tomorrow?"

"It's urgent," Winter replied. "It's about Shea," he added, just to get his point across.

"Very well then," Skylar said, his tone suddenly all business. "Follow me. We'll talk in the office."

With that, Skylar headed back into the house. The office was one of the few locations in the Cunningham mansion that Winter avoided. The two shifters hadn't explicitly told him he needed to stay away, but most official business took place here, so Winter only ever came around if explicitly invited. After all, he was technically speaking still a stranger.

Skylar didn't ask any questions or make any comment as they walked. In fact, he didn't speak at all, which was unusual of the seahorse. It made Winter nervous, and he squeezed Corbin's hand tighter, finding anchor in the lynx's strength.

Finally, they reached their destination and, of course, found Byron already waiting there. "What's this you want to tell us about Shea?" the shark asked without preamble as his mate closed the office door.

Winter swallowed around the sudden knot in his throat. This was it. He finally had to face his choices and his lies.

"My name is Winter Tomacelli, and I am the heir for the Sidhe throne. My uncle, the current king, sent me here to steal Shea. I have no idea what he wants with the baby, but he is insisting on me taking him back to the palace as soon as possible." He spoke as quickly as possible, not knowing when Byron would cut him off. "I've tried to stall, but there's nothing more I can do. He gave me two days before he brands me as a traitor. Once that happens, I expect he will send someone else to retrieve Shea. I'm sorry I didn't tell you any of this before, but I was worried you wouldn't believe me or you'd hate me. I never once wanted to separate Shea from Layton and Preston. I swear it."

He waited for a reaction, but none came. Finally, Byron gave him a cool look and inquired, "Is that all?"

"In a nutshell," Winter replied, somehow managing to keep his voice steady.

"All right then." Byron got up from his desk, his large figure looking more imposing as ever. "Now, I'd like to ask you one question."

"Please do." Winter was willing to answer any questions Byron had. After all, he'd deceived the man for over a year. The Cunninghams deserved a little honesty now.

"Do you consider Skylar and me idiots?"

Winter gave the shark a blank look. Was that a rhetorical question? Was he expected to answer? Clearly, Byron didn't believe him because otherwise, why would he ask such a thing?

Before he could come up with a coherent reply, Skylar offered the answer to his dilemma. "Winter, did you really think Byron and I would allow you or any other stranger next to Shea without investigating his or her purpose here? Of course we knew why you'd been sent in our home. It wasn't even hard to guess with the offer your king made us. We were just biding our time to see what you would do."

Byron shook his head, his lips twisting into a smirk. "I don't know what your king was thinking. Did he really believe we'd forget about the offer he made and not make the connection with your stay here?"

In truth, Winter had asked himself the same question many times and had concluded that the shifters were too self-assured to believe one Sidhe could breach their defenses. His mind went hazy. All this time, he'd been agonizing over what to do, and they'd known. They'd watched him. How could they have been so cold? Surely they must have realized how much the situation irked him.

Even so, he knew he had no right to feel slighted. He'd been the one to deceive the Cunninghams first, and even if they had expected it, that didn't justify his own deed. He bit his lip as hard as he could to suppress the feeling of acute humiliation coursing through him and asked, "So now what? I can't keep him from trying to take Shea."

"Of course you can." Skylar started looking through the office library and retrieved a tome. Much to Winter's dismay, it looked a lot like a copy of the Sidhe Sacred Law, the equivalent of their constitution. It was an ancient piece of legislation, and of course Skylar couldn't have the original volume. That particular tome was encased in thick, enchanted glass in the Sidhe palace library. But either way, seeing the book in Skylar's hands surprised Winter. What piece of information could the Sacred Law keep that would help them in their predicament?

"Our main problem isn't that Sterling wants Shea, but that Sterling is the Sidhe king. If you were to take the throne, his power would be gone and the threat neutralized."

"That's true," Winter answered, "but I'm not old enough to seize the crown. I need to at least reach my thirtieth year and my maturity as Sidhe."

"There is a way around that," Skylar answered. "Come now. You must know what I mean. You're royalty. You must have studied the law extensively."

Dread coursed through Winter. "No." He shook his head resolutely. "Absolutely not. You would have me wed my own uncle? That's folly."

He felt Corbin's shock at his proclamation, and even Skylar seemed a bit taken aback. Perhaps he hadn't realized the true meaning of the law he'd mentioned.

"What in the world?" Corbin asked, speaking for the first time since they'd entered the office. "What do you mean wed him?"

"We Sidhe have always been a very conservative people. Many of us are still purists to this day. A long time ago, when the Sacred Law was written, this tendency was taken to the extreme. There is a proviso in the oldest texts that allows for inbreeding between relations, and even encourages it, especially amongst royalty. One particular point of the same law was that if the heir of a throne is too young, the eldest of his close relatives will act as a king until his coming of age. However, if the heir in question were to wed an older relation, he would be able to become king and take the crown in spite of his age."

"This copy of the Sacred Law doesn't mention you wedding Sterling. The translator must have gotten in wrong."

"But it must have mentioned a wedding of sorts anyway," Corbin protested. "How can you even suggest something like that? Winter never meant any harm. He is family now."

"Corbin, I understand your point, but now is not the time for such emotions," Byron replied. "As much as we appreciate Winter for his own merits, we will never surrender Shea, and that means war. If Winter can do something to prevent it, I would expect him to make the sacrifice and act."

In a way, Winter agreed with Byron. He'd always known that as royalty, he'd be expected to marry one day, but even so, he'd foolishly hoped it would be for love and not an arrangement. Byron was right. Feelings didn't matter here. Facts did.

"That might be true," he replied, "but my uncle would never marry me. There's simply no way."

"And it would defeat the very purpose of the arrangement." Skylar hummed thoughtfully. "Is there anyone else you can wed?"

Winter thought hard, considering the rest of his family tree. Most of his older relatives were already married, and those single didn't like him very much. He thought that he might have a cousin that would be willing, but he hadn't seen the man in five years. He didn't know if the guy had taken a partner or not.

"I'd have to look into it," he replied, doing his best not to think about what he was agreeing to. He felt horrible about this whole thing, especially with Corbin standing right there. Why couldn't Corbin be Sidhe? Winter would gladly marry him.

Winter shook himself, shelving that thought in a corner of his mind reserved for impossible dreams. Corbin deserved better than to be thrust into a world of political intrigue. Besides, the lynx might care about him, but the responsibility of a king's consort was overwhelming even for a Sidhe. Not to mention that such a position carried a lot of danger. The Unseelie rogues were forever attempting to overthrow the reigning royal family, and for a shifter to get into that sort of thing was pure madness.

Why was he even thinking about it? It could not be. The best thing he could do was to contact his cousin. The Sidhe had long ago stopped marrying their kin, but the man would probably agree just the same. After all, there was no law saying they actually had to consummate their union. They could both have lovers on the side if they so desired. Personally, Winter couldn't imagine loving sharing his body with anyone except Corbin, and he'd never force the lynx into being a side dish.

All these thoughts whirled in his mind, and he knew he wasn't being very coherent in response to Skylar's query. "There is one man who might accept," he finally managed to say, "but I'm not absolutely certain."

"Over my dead body." Corbin's voice was low and dangerous. "You're not marrying anyone else but me."

Winter turned toward Corbin, shocked beyond words. It was as if the lynx had read his mind and his desires. But Byron was, as always, the voice of cold reason. "It doesn't work like that, Corbin."

"Oh?" Corbin arched a brow. "And why not? If feelings weren't involved, why didn't you just give Shea away and save us all the trouble?"

Both Cunninghams tensed visibly. "Corbin, what are you saying?" Skylar asked, sounding shocked. "We could never do something like that."

"Of course you couldn't," Corbin shot back. "You wouldn't ask your children to make such a sacrifice. Personally, I agree wholeheartedly. And yet you're asking Winter to do something that is at least comparable, if not similar. How can you look at us in the face and say feelings have no place in politics when this whole conflict is based on emotions?"

Winter couldn't believe the things Corbin was saying to the Cunninghams on his account. The two older shifters remained silent while Corbin continued to rant, "You two are like family, and I've respected you all my life. I never thought I would one day call you hypocrites, but right now, that's what you are."

Corbin seemed on a roll, and God only knew what the lynx would say next if Winter didn't stop him. "Stop, Corbin, please," he murmured. "It's hardly the same thing. Shea is their grandson. I'm just a stranger."

"That's just it," Corbin answered, his voice frustrated. "You're not a stranger, not after one year of being with me. With us."

The "me" meant more than Corbin himself probably knew. As long as Corbin cared for him, Winter truly felt like he wasn't a stranger here. To his surprise, Corbin's heartfelt words reached out the Cunninghams, as well.

"You're right, Corbin," Skylar said. "But you must understand we cannot be objective where Layton and Morgan are concerned."

"Of course I understand," Corbin answered. "I never asked you to. I trust your judgment. But I can't accept this double standard set against Winter."

"Well, this leaves us in quite a quandary," Skylar said. "Unless..." The seahorse shared a look with his shark mate. They were obviously talking in that way that only mates could.

"Unless what?" Winter prodded.

"Our sources say that your uncle never explicitly told your people you were here," Byron said with a small smile. "I expect he wouldn't have liked to explain why he was deliberately sending off the heir to the throne into danger."

"Well, since my parents were assassinated, it was considered too dangerous for me to remain at the palace." The continuous reminder of his parents' murder made a cold chill flow through Winter. "I only rarely visited, and me being missing for one year would not surprise anyone."

"Well, we can use all that," Byron said, "if you're willing, of course."

Winter was beginning to get a headache. "Use it how?"

"You said you didn't want to wed your kin, and we agreed that it was an unreasonable request on our part," Skylar said. "But what if you married a shifter instead? Like Corbin so eloquently put it, what if you married him?"

Winter felt like the two shifters were playing ping-pong with his brain. "But…You said it yourself, that wouldn't help."

"Not for the purpose of you getting the throne, no." Skylar seemed thoughtful, as if musing over this new plan. "But with some work, we can present it as a new alliance between shifters and Sidhe. Your uncle never mentioned the conflict between us, and your stay here, when it is revealed, will be an argument for the preparation of that alliance."

It was hard to believe that just a few moments earlier, Winter had been considering this exact same thing in terms of an impossible wish. The Cunninghams seemed to believe it was a valid solution, but Winter honestly didn't know if they could pull it off.

"It will never work," he said. "He won't allow it."

"Oh, he'll have no choice." Skylar's grin was wicked. "I can guarantee you that." His expression sobered. "But I don't want to push you again. If you're against this, or if Corbin is, we'll find something else. After all, Corbin is right. You are no longer a stranger here."

Skylar's words might have soothed Winter somewhat, except they came too late. Winter's mind was already screaming a litany of anxious nos. And it wasn't even because he didn't want to belong to Corbin. God help him, there was nothing he wanted more. But doing it this way, wedding Corbin for political purposes, it made the entire thing seem so cheap and tawdry. Winter had never even allowed himself to spend too much time with the lynx, worried that he'd give too much away or, more importantly, he'd allow himself to fall for the shifter. This meant that, sadly, in spite of their instinctual attraction and the genuine caring between them, they truly knew very little about each other.

Not only that, but the situation brought Winter to his previous concern. Accepting such an idea would involve Corbin in dangerous Sidhe politics. The mere thought of having Corbin risk his life this way made Winter sick to his stomach.

"I...I'll agree to it, but only if Corbin wants to," he replied. "Marriage into the Sidhe royal family isn't exactly something easy to handle."

"I can handle more than you think, sweetheart," Corbin replied. He'd never once let go of Winter's hand throughout the conversation, but now, his arm went around Winter's waist, pulling him close. "Just don't let them bully you into anything," he whispered in Winter's ear. "I'm here, whether we are mated or not."

Warmth flooded Winter upon feeling Corbin's body against his own. Suddenly, his apprehension began to be overshadowed by arousal. His mind knew this was a serious situation, but his libido wanted a continuation of what they'd begun earlier.

"I know," he replied, "and you have no idea how much I appreciate it. I just don't want you to be in danger." He'd already lost two loved ones to the Unseelie. He couldn't bear the thought of it happening again.

Corbin caressed Winter's face and lips almost reverently. "Don't worry, sweetheart. I'll be fine. You won't ever lose me. I promise." His almost somber tone turned naughty. "Seal the deal with a kiss?"

Winter couldn't have refused to save his life. Lost in Corbin's blue gaze, he surrendered to Corbin's strength. When Corbin pressed their mouths together, Winter was assaulted by a feeling of rightness that pushed aside all the doubts.

Parting his lips, Winter allowed the other man entry. He wrapped his arms around Corbin's neck, melting into the lynx's embrace. How could he possibly resist this? How could he even think about giving it up?

It was only when they broke apart to breathe that Winter realized the Cunninghams were still in the room. He felt himself flush as he turned toward Skylar and Byron.

"I guess that's a yes," Skylar said, a light, good-natured smile on his lips.

Winter nodded. "I suppose." Corbin's scent was distracting as hell, and he knew he was forgetting about something.

When Corbin nibbled on his neck, Winter pushed away from the lynx. "Give me a minute, okay? We have to…ah…What did I want to say?"

Corbin obediently stayed put, and Winter managed to gather his thoughts. "Right. If Corbin and I are to be married, it'll have to be by the Sidhe ways, too. That will imply a special garb, which I can only get from the palace, as well as the participation of one of our priests."

"I expected that much. Don't worry. We don't mean to keep the wedding a secret from the king. We'll just mention it in the right ears before we tell him. Byron and I haven't been idle in the past year. We've prepared ourselves for all possible outcomes, including a war."

Looking at Skylar's face, Winter wondered what in the world he'd gotten himself into. Clearly, Skylar had more than one card up his sleeve. It was quite likely that King Sterling would end up in a poor position because of Winter's choice. His uncle would be furious once he found out about this. But as he leaned against Corbin, Winter thought it just might be worth it.

Chapter Four

There was nothing King Sterling Tomacelli hated more than being forced into a certain course of action. He'd always appreciated freedom, something which, sadly, people from the royal family never benefited from. But what irked him more was that what little freedom he did have had been taken from his hands by a higher power.

The Oracle gave him a kind, yet stern look with her sightless eyes. When she spoke, her lips didn't move. "Things are in motion, King Sterling. Your envoy has not accomplished his task, and the future that we attempted to build is gone."

Sterling sighed. A part of him didn't regret that too much, but he knew it was unfair. He had a responsibility to his late brother, a responsibility to protect Winter, even from himself. Unfortunately, he couldn't exactly explain that to Winter as the existence of the Oracle represented a well-guarded secret only the king and his consort were privy to. She did not even have a physical manifestation, but rather, was more like a banshee, giving the current leader of the nation the gift of foresight. And Winter would never believe him if Sterling said he'd suddenly had a vision from the Gods.

Not to mention that his dear nephew had become resentful because Sterling had taken over the throne. Sterling wished he could have been kinder with Winter, given him more affection after his brother had died, but circumstances had not allowed it. Winter looked so much like his parents that it was very hard for Sterling to even be in his presence, not to mention that the hostile elements who'd been behind the assassination of the two royals still existed. Those who'd actually killed the two had been dealt with, but the brains of the operation had never been found.

"Advise me, Great One," he told the Oracle, the pain inside him growing as he looked at her sweet face. "What should I do? I don't want Winter to suffer."

"I know you don't. Sending him to the shifters was a good first step, and while his choices will carry him down a dark path, he will be loved. " She gave him a look full of caring and compassion. "For as long as he lives."

"Is there no way to avoid it, Oracle?"

"Had you wed Shea Cunningham, Winter would have been spared that pain. But the future is not yet completely written. I can see the darkness of his death, but it is clouded. I do not know its source. You must stand by his side now and support him in any way you can. Your future, and his, are not lost."

Sterling rubbed his eyes tiredly. "I should have never told him to steal Shea. He'll never trust me now."

The Oracle offered him a small smile. "Be patient. His choice earned him a place in the shifter household. It would have been better if he'd retrieved the child, yes, or rather, safer. But there is still hope. Do not despair."

Even with the Oracle's encouragement, it was hard to keep composure when he knew how badly he'd failed Winter. The Sidhe was so young and had no idea what filth hid behind the façade of royalty. Alas, Sterling had to keep of the pretense of aloofness and purism. If he didn't, royal blood or not, he would end up like his elder brother. And then where would Winter be?

Sterling clung to the thought that the Oracle would not lie to him and nodded. She was right. He could not surrender the battle. His brother was watching over him from the beyond and depended on Sterling to protect Winter. He had to believe there was a way out of every path and around every future.

"Very well, Great One," he said. "Thank you for all your help. I will start preparations for his wedding now."

"One more thing," she added. "When you go to him, pay close attention. The shifters will hate you, and the Cunninghams in particular will try to make your life difficult. But the walls have ears in their home. There is only one person you can trust absolutely, outside yourself. Corbin Mckenna. He can help you protect Winter."

Corbin. The lynx shifter who'd stolen Winter's heart. Perhaps not all was lost. If Winter had made a good choice regarding his life partner, Sterling couldn't believe fate would be so cruel so as to end Winter's existence too early.

The Oracle's blind eyes suddenly turned their natural green, and her translucent hair became red as flame. Her voice no longer sounded so outlandish when she spoke. "Come now, Sterling," she said softly. "I know you can do it. I'm relying on you to help my son."

"Oh, Jayna..." Sterling was hard pressed not to cry. "I've failed you."

"No, you haven't," she replied. "There's still time. Bringing Shea here was the right solution, but it was unlikely that the shifters would agree. We knew it before even trying." Her kind expression turned into a frown. "I don't want to see you gloomy anymore. I know you'll be able to find the solution. After all, you're the King of the Sidhe."

Oh, if only she were right. But Sterling had been unable to stop her death and that of his brother, Lamont. The two people he'd most loved in his entire existence, and they were gone, just like that. He'd been so grief stricken that only the knowledge of Winter's vulnerability had given him strength to move on.

His surprise had been great when Jayna had come to him as the Oracle. He knew now that each Oracle was different, according to generations, and Jayna had taken up this role, reluctant to leave her people and her son adrift. Even now, she was so beautiful, the same woman Sterling had loved with an all-consuming passion but had surrendered to Lamont when his brother had wanted her as his wife. He'd have fought for her love, except he knew that Jayna felt the same way Lamont did. And so he had supported their marriage, and when Winter had been conceived, he'd loved the child as his own.

"Well, I should depart now," Jayna said. Her not-quite-ghostly hand extended, revealing a small pendant. "Take this. It is a wedding present for Winter and a token of my love. Thank you again, Sterling. Lamont and I will never forget it."

Sterling took the pendant. For a few seconds, it felt light as a feather in his palm, as if it wasn't quite there. But as those moments passed, it materialized, becoming a crystal gem in the shape of a teardrop. When he looked up from the jewel, Jayna had returned to her original Oracle appearance. "It will be as you say, Great One," Sterling promised. "We won't allow for anything different."

The Oracle, or rather Jayna, nodded. "Farewell for now, King Sterling. We will see each other soon. And don't forget, Shea is the key."

And with that, she disappeared into thin air, leaving Sterling with the teardrop pendant as the only tangible evidence she'd been there at all. It was better than other times, when she vanished almost without warning, often making Sterling question his own sanity.

However, there was one thing Sterling didn't question now. He needed to make haste and help prepare Winter's wedding. He had no idea when the threat to Winter's life would appear or how Shea would be involved. Not even the Oracle could see all things. It would be up to Sterling to be ready for what she hadn't mentioned.

The next couple of hours were a blur of giving orders to the royal tailors and jewel craftsmen and making sure the rest of his tasks were done, so that he'd be prepared when the time came for departure. He also double-checked some of the information the Oracle had given him. According to her, the Cunninghams had somehow managed the elves and the sprites. Sterling knew the elders of these nations personally, and he didn't think any clash would exist between them.

The relationships with the vampire coven and merfolk were a bit more strained, but nothing that could not be handled. Of course, Sterling wondered how in the world the Cunninghams had gotten over the fact that a siren had essentially cursed their youngest son so easily. In some things, the shifters were a mystery to him.

At the same time, Sterling was curious as to how Skylar Cunningham meant to pull off a wedding where so many different people would be invited. It was clear that Winter needed Sterling there since the day of his marriage would rapidly turn into just a political event without his intervention.

A few hours after his conversation with Jayna, the shifter he'd been studying finally contacted him. Sterling's assistant announced an incoming call from Skylar Cunningham, and Sterling took it on his personal line. Sidhe might be conservative creatures, but they still owned phones. When he activated the connection, Skylar's face popped up on the vid screen.

"Greetings, Your Majesty," the shifter said politely. "I'm glad to see you so well."

Sterling suppressed a grimace. Skylar's voice was empty of any deception or irony, but Sterling knew better than to believe the seahorse held any fond sentiment for him. He had no patience for schemes now or for the shifter trying to be a smart-ass.

"And good tidings to you as well, Mr. Cunningham," he replied. "I trust you are calling about Winter's wedding?"

A brief flicker of surprise flashed over Skylar's face before the seahorse quickly masked it. "Indeed." He released a small laugh. "It seems the proverbial cat is out of the bag. I'd hoped to give you the good news myself."

"Well, you didn't expect me to leave Winter alone with no supervision for one year, right?" He arched a brow at Skylar, secretly amused at making the seahorse worry about his security. In fact, it might not hurt if the Cunninghams added a few more guards. It could actually help save Winter. "Not that I don't trust you to keep him safe, but as his closest kin, I am entitled to watch over him."

"Of course." Nothing in Skylar's tone of expression revealed what he thought about Sterling's words. "I assume you know we'll be having many distinguished guests."

"Quite," Sterling replied. "I'm making preparations as we speak for Winter to look exactly like what he is. Royalty."

For the first time, Skylar beamed, and Sterling actually thought the smile genuine. He was struck by how beautiful that expression made the seahorse. Shaking himself, he focused on the conversation. "That's excellent," the seahorse said. "Winter has told us a lot about Sidhe traditions, but we'd never be able to achieve such a ceremony without your aid."

Sterling supposed the comment was meant as a temporary olive branch and decided to take it. "I have my men working on what is needed as we speak. I will be flying into Los Angeles tonight if that's all right with you."

"That's perfect," Skylar replied. "We will be honored to have you."

"And now, if I may, could I speak to my nephew? I'm sure he must be around there somewhere."

Sterling had anticipated a refusal from Skylar's part, but the seahorse just summoned Winter. The younger Sidhe appeared on the vid screen, looking a bit pale, but decided. "Hello, Uncle," he said.

"Hello, Winter." Sterling offered Winter a small smile. "I hear congratulations are in order."

Winter nodded, seeming just a touch apprehensive. "Thank you. I'm very happy."

"I'm glad to hear that. Like I mentioned to Mr. Cunningham, your suit is already being prepared. I will be making further arrangements with your hosts. As it is the wedding of our prince and future king, it needs to be done with full pomp. I advise you to discuss our rites with your soon-to-be husband and teach him his vows."

Now, Winter looked fully taken aback. "Yes, Uncle. Of course. You don't have to worry about that."

"Excellent. Congratulations again, my boy. I'll see you in a couple of hours."

Winter still appeared to be lost in disbelief when Sterling returned to his conversation with Skylar. He hadn't lied. Further arrangements needed to be made, and Sterling still had to notify the shifters of the content of his party.

Later that day, after everything that could be dealt with here had been arranged, Sterling went to the Temple of the Silver Pool. It was the grand prelate of the temple that officiated all important weddings. Usually, the prelate was forbidden to leave Sidhe territory, but Sterling decided an exception needed to be made in this case. He'd have preferred it if Winter married in his palace, as he should have, but the shifters who'd started this whole thing were unlikely to agree.

"But are you certain, Your Majesty?" the man asked, sounding a bit put out at Sterling's order. Sterling couldn't blame him. The grand prelate hadn't left the palace in over three decades. Some days, Sterling was surprised the priest even remembered how to walk.

"Are you questioning me?" Sterling arched a brow. The prelate shook his head but looked like he intended to protest further. Sterling decided to save himself the trouble and emphasize the importance of the situation. "Very good," he added. "I wouldn't want to have to choose a different grand prelate on the eve of my nephew's wedding."

That essentially shut the man up. *Now, to the more important business.* Leaving the grand prelate to worry about living his comfortable existence, Sterling headed into the temple.

The Silver Pool was, essentially, the core of energy all Sidhe had. Its symbol and the wellspring of Sidhe magic was the large pond in the middle of the temple. Its pure, clean waters were said to be able to heal all afflictions. It was in this temple that Winter had received most of his instruction as a healer, and here Sterling hoped to find help for whatever came.

The temple adepts met him at the door, bowing at him and gesturing him forward. Sterling followed their silent advice and stepped toward the pool. As he knelt next to the glowing pond, he found his mind clearing and his despair melting into renewed decision. When he got up, he knew that no matter what he had to do, he would save Winter from his fate.

Chapter Five

"Tell me that again. I could have sworn you just said you're mating Winter Tomacelli in two days."

Corbin suppressed the urge to fidget under Nicolas's displeased gaze. So far, his adoptive dad had been nice to Winter, and Corbin had hoped to find some support there for telling his father. Garth was still not quite over the injury Nicolas had suffered in Elder Adele Mercier's attack. While he'd never treated Winter poorly because of it, Corbin doubted his father would be pleased.

There were so many things he could say to convince Nicolas that he truly wanted to become Winter's mate. However, he still didn't have things one hundred percent clear in his head. Oh, he was convinced this was the right thing to do. His inner beast couldn't be happier at the knowledge that Winter would soon be his. But at the same time, there were still so many questions on his mind. How would he, a shifter, manage to be the consort of the future Sidhe king? Corbin could deal with the responsibilities of the position, but would he be accepted?

More importantly, did Winter feel the same thing Corbin did, or was he only marrying Corbin because he had no choice?

In the end, Corbin sighed and said, "He's my mate, Dad. I'm not sure he realizes it since I haven't told him. Our connection is there, but it's not easy to build a relationship when you're knee-deep in political intrigue."

"Fair enough." Nicolas eyed Corbin, as if assessing his honesty. "I believe you, and I do like Winter. However, not everyone's going to be so accepting."

Corbin plopped down on the couch and buried his face in his hands. "I know. Please, Dad, help me. We're making the announcement tonight before all the guests leave. I don't want to make a mess of Preston's wedding day, so I'm worried."

"Of course you can count on my help," Nicolas replied. "What did Skylar say?"

Corbin couldn't exactly tell his adoptive dad that it had been largely the Cunninghams' idea in the first place. Nicolas would probably interpret it the wrong way. "He agrees it's best to make haste."

"Okay. Now, brace yourself. Here comes your father."

Corbin suppressed a grimace. This was the problem with telling Nicolas about his impending wedding. Because of his bond with Garth, Nicolas couldn't hide anything from the older lynx. Corbin did not feel at all prepared to face his father.

Moments later, Garth burst into the room, an expression of barely veiled anger on his face. "Just tell me this isn't a part of some harebrained scheme of Byron's. Just tell me that, and I'll be happy."

"It isn't," Corbin said. It wasn't a lie since he truly did want Winter to be his mate. "It's true that they are encouraging it for political purposes, but he really is my mate. You know this, Father. You've seen me with him."

Garth's shoulders slumped. "I suppose you're right." He sounded defeated. "I don't dislike Winter. He's a good boy. But he's also royal blood, and that will bring you far too many problems. I wanted something different for you."

It was a pleasant surprise to hear Garth wasn't against the wedding because of Winter being a Sidhe, but rather, due to the implications of the Sidhe being a prince and future king. Even if Corbin shared his concerns, he decided he could deal with them when the time came.

"I can handle it," he told his father. "Now, I want you guys to be ready. We're telling everyone tonight, at dinner, before the guests leave. I have to go talk to Winter. I'll see you in a bit, all right?"

His parents let him go, and Corbin headed out of the room to find his mate. It was striking how easy it had become for him to think of Winter like that. He followed his instincts and found Winter still in Byron's office, together with Skylar.

"We just got off the phone with my uncle," Winter said. "He is—"

Their eyes met, and Winter suddenly stopped speaking. It was as if they were lost in each other's gazes. Distantly, Corbin noted the moment when Skylar discreetly took his leave. Taking advantage of their new privacy, Corbin approached the Sidhe.

"Tell me, sweetheart. What were you going to say?"

"My uncle is actually supportive of us. I'm surprised. He even seemed to know about everything Mr. Cunningham did."

Corbin mused over Winter's words, all the while noting how much he liked hearing the word *us* from Winter's lips. Still, he needed to address the most pressing concern on his mind. "We can still call it off if you're not sure," he told the Sidhe. "Your uncle won't do anything now that he knows we have foreign backing."

"I really don't know." Winter sighed. "This is all so confusing. Just a few hours ago, I knew where I stood. But now…God, it's too much."

Corbin felt for the younger man. Since the decision had been made, everything had turned into a whirlwind, until Corbin had completely lost direction and forgotten why they were doing this in the first place. It was as if he'd become a leaf whirled around in a tornado, involved in issues that were far too big for him to fully comprehend.

But Corbin wanted to understand. He wanted to be the mate Winter needed. "Do you trust your uncle?" he asked.

"Not really, no," Winter replied. "I still don't know why marrying Shea was so important to him, especially since Shea is only a baby."

Winter gave Corbin an almost desperate look. "God, Corbin, I don't want to involve you in this mess, too."

There was no point in saying Corbin had become involved ever since he'd set eyes on Winter. That wouldn't make the sweet fae feel any better. Instead, Corbin wrapped his arms around Winter and kissed the Sidhe's forehead. "We'll be fine as long as we stick together. It's all very confusing now, yes. But our marriage is supposed to cement an age-old alliance, something your uncle won't be able to block." He paused for effect and added, "And personally, I'm quite happy being your mate. If you'll have me."

"Oh, Corbin. Why are you being so great about this?" Winter asked. "You should hate me for messing up your life, for lying, for pushing you away."

Corbin arched a brow. "It almost sounds that you want me to hate you."

"Of course not." Winter looked away, seemingly troubled. "I just…I'm sorry. I really don't know how to handle all this."

"How about we start from the beginning?" Corbin suggested. "If we go by Mr. Cunningham's suggestions, we're going to have to get married soon. So teach me everything I need to know so I don't embarrass myself, or you. I learned a few things as basic education, but it's hardly enough."

"You're right." The task seemed to center Winter as the Sidhe suddenly looked more collected. "We're very keen on ceremonies, so we'll start with that. Okay?"

"That's fine with me, sweetheart."

Winter smiled at him, and Corbin's heart melted. For Winter's sake, he would learn ten different languages if he had to. Having Winter as his teacher would just be an excellent plus.

* * * *

That evening, the entire family gathered, prepared for everything. The guests had been told there would be an important announcement later that evening, but no one except close friends knew what it really entailed.

The Cunninghams were of the opinion that Corbin and Winter should remain separated until that moment, but Corbin decided against it. He wanted to spend as much time as he could with Winter now that it had become accepted.

"Do you think they'll take it well?" Winter asked in a whisper.

Corbin shrugged. "Maybe, maybe not. But I think that eventually, everyone will realize this is a good thing. Twenty years ago, no one would have thought shifters could live in peace with each other, but now it's true. Sure, we don't always get along, but we're not actively at war, either. Openness toward other species is the natural next step, and having Sidhe as allies is amazing progress."

Just minutes before the actual event, Isaac and their swan friend, Reed, discreetly joined them. "I hear you're making plans to join the ranks of the traitors," Isaac commented.

Corbin was startled by the comment until he saw the look on Isaac's face. "That's right," he replied cheekily, "and quite happily so."

"Our parents haven't stopped badgering us all day." Reed sighed, his eyes scanning the crowd as if he were looking for someone. "Seems we're the only ones without stable relationships."

"What about Melanie, Jace, and Derek?" Corbin inquired. He'd seen the three werewolves earlier, and to his knowledge, they weren't involved with anyone, either.

"They're all dating people." Isaac sighed. "Maybe you and I should date each other, Reed."

Reed's horrified look would have been amusing had it not seemed so honest. "I guess the answer's no, huh?" Isaac asked with a grin. "We'll just have to suffer together."

"For the moment, hang around us," Winter suggested. "With this news, we'll be the center of attention and your parents will stop their insistence for a while."

Reed didn't seem convinced but nevertheless hung around. They fell into comfortable conversation, and Corbin marveled at how well Winter fit in with his friends. He had to constantly remind himself not to wrap an arm around Winter and pull him close. It just felt so comfortable and right.

He was almost relieved when the moment of the announcement finally came. Everyone seemed to expect something from Preston or Morgan, perhaps the arrival of another child. But no such thing happened.

"On this joyous day," Skylar said, "we have more excellent news. I'll leave Corbin to tell you the rest."

Corbin was known to everyone mostly because he'd helped out his father with the Agency. Other than that, he was by no means a preeminent figure like Skylar or Byron. He felt somewhat out of his depth when all eyes turned to him but didn't let it show. After all, once he wed Winter, he'd have much more difficult things to do and announce.

"First of all," he started, "I'd like to thank you all for being here to celebrate with us. Both my brother and my family and friends appreciate it greatly. For that reason, I am happy to share one of the greatest things in my life with you. Today, I asked Winter Tomacelli to become my mate, and he accepted."

Things hadn't gone exactly like that, but they didn't need to know every detail. Murmurs of surprise swept over the crowd, several of the guests looking completely gobsmacked. No one was actually saying a word out loud, though. Corbin didn't think that this was very promising.

And then, somewhere from the back, Clark's voice came, loud and clear. "Woohoo!" the lion roared. "Way to go, Corb!"

"You go, Corbin," Clark's mate, Angel, echoed. "Congrats!"

Alexis was the next one to intervene. "Congrats, Winter," the incubus echoed, this time addressing the comment to the Sidhe.

Corbin could have kissed them for their initiative. In a way, it didn't surprise him. Clark and Angel had suffered some backlash because their mating was considered, in a way, taboo. Alexis wasn't much better off as incubi were generally seen as heartless whores. They understood Corbin and Winter, and their help meant a lot.

After that, more voices joined the first ones. Corbin mentally thanked his family and friends, who were so supportive. True, they'd been told ahead of time, but they'd also showed a lot of enthusiasm.

Once they saw the general attitude, the other guests started to get into the groove, too. They came and congratulated Corbin and Winter. They were still a little awkward around the Sidhe, but Winter took it all with a smile, charming them in a way Corbin could never have attempted.

And then, just as everyone was starting to relax, Skylar and Byron signaled at Corbin to get ready. Corbin shared a look with Winter, who nodded. "Don't worry," Corbin mouthed. "We'll be fine."

He wished he could have said more, perhaps an "I love you" like Winter deserved. But there simply wasn't time. Before he knew it, the Sidhe delegation made their appearance. Corbin had expected it, and still, they startled him. It wasn't their arrival per se that shocked him, but rather the way they looked. Dressed in what must have been traditional Sidhe finery, they practically glittered. At the same time, however, they seemed so aloof, so distant and unlike Winter that Corbin balked at the task of getting them to like him.

Shrugging to himself, Corbin decided they might look glamorous, but that didn't make them better than him. He could handle whatever they threw at him. It would be somewhat more difficult with the current king, but Sterling would not be able to hold onto his crown for love. Corbin didn't really want to be king of anything, but it was Winter's birthright, and Corbin would make sure his sweetheart got anything he wanted.

For the moment, though, Sterling was king, and as such, needed to be greeted with full pomp. Together with the Cunninghams, Corbin accompanied Winter to see to the Sidhe delegation.

Corbin had never actually met Sterling Tomacelli before, and it surprised him to see that the Sidhe king was actually much younger than Corbin had expected. Or perhaps he just looked that way. For all his youthful appearance, his eyes held a very old look.

"Hello, Your Majesty," Winter said, bowing. Corbin followed his example, even if the only thing he wanted was to kick Sterling in the face.

"Please rise, nephew," Sterling said. "And this must be your intended. It is a pleasure to meet you, Mr. Mckenna."

"The pleasure is all mine," Corbin said with a tight smile. "Winter has told me so much about you."

"I'm sure." Sterling smiled back, somehow managing to make the expression look both pleasant and condescending.

Thankfully, Skylar intervened before the situation could get nasty. "We are honored to have you here," he told Sterling. "Please, step this way. Would you like me to show you around?"

"Thank you, Mr. Cunningham," the Sidhe king replied. "I'd like that very much." Before he left, however, he said to Winter, "Congratulations on your engagement, nephew. You and I will talk later in more detail."

To Corbin, those words sounded ominous, and he glowered at Sterling's back as the Sidhe began to walk away.

"It's okay," Winter whispered in his ear. "He was actually much more pleasant than I thought he'd be."

Corbin supposed Winter meant to soothe him, but it didn't quite work. He couldn't help but wonder what exactly counted as unpleasantness for Sidhe. Clearly, Corbin would have to learn to have ice flowing through his veins if he meant to be the future consort of the Sidhe king.

Chapter Six

A few days later

Winter looked into the mirror, scanning his own reflection with a critical eye. The outfit his uncle had deigned to bring was, well, made for a king. Woven from a thread of pure silver using the ancient crafts of the fae, it folded around Winter in several layers. Tradition spoke that as the ceremony progressed, he would shed more and more of the clothing, until at last, during their wedding night, he would be naked. Sadly, the entire proceedings, including the party to celebrate the event, always took a long, long time, especially for Sidhe with high titles. This meant that the more important the Sidhe was, the more layers his or her outfit would have. For Winter, his garb had no less than twelve layers, one for each age in Sidhe history. If not for the skill of Sidhe tailors, Winter would probably look twice his size and be sweating like a pig.

Winter turned toward his only companion and asked, "How do I look?"

Alexis snickered at him. "Don't fish for compliments. You know you look great." The demon made his way to Winter's side and caressed the lapel of Winter's shirt. "Your uncle really outdid himself. God, I could come just by touching this material."

Winter slapped the incubus's hand away. "Leave my clothing out of your dirty fantasies. Does Morgan know you have such fetishes?"

The demon laughed gaily. "Oh, he knows, and he loves to indulge me." His expression sobered a bit. "Sorry I'm such a nutcase today. I never thought people could be more agitated than the day of my mating, but compared to this, that party was nothing. There's just so much emotion it's unbearable."

Quite honestly, Winter agreed with the incubus. With the elders of so many different species present, the potential for discontent was astounding, and more so since some species had been involved in attacks on shifters before. The merfolk leader had been unexpectedly open and had punished the siren guilty of attacking Preston and Layton the year before. The warlocks hadn't been so nice, or at least, not to Winter's knowledge. But they weren't actively hostile, and that was always something.

Winter shook himself, forcing his mind away from issues of foreign politics. This was his wedding, and he would enjoy it. "Do you think Corbin will like the way I look?" he asked Alexis.

"Oh, he'll have trouble not ripping those lovely clothes off." Alexis beamed. "Stop worrying. Corbin cares about you deeply. Just enjoy your special day."

It was easy for Alexis to say. The incubus had become Morgan's official mate a year after they'd actually bonded. By then they even had a child and everyone accepted the process as normal and expected. This was entirely different, and Winter knew that not everyone close to the family was so accepting as Alexis.

He took a deep breath and struggled for calm. Truly, if he left aside all the political machinations, he wanted this. Perhaps he and Corbin needed to elope.

Winter was deeply considering this new idea when a knock sounded at the door. He groaned, already knowing who was on the other side. Alexis gave him an inquiring look, to which Winter just nodded. There was no point avoiding this conversation. He'd known it would come.

Without a word, Alexis opened the door and allowed Sterling in. He greeted Winter's uncle respectfully, as befitting the Sidhe king's station, then turned toward Winter. "I'll step outside for a moment to check on Elian. I'll be right back."

With that, Alexis took his leave, abandoning Winter to his fate. Winter forced himself to smile at his royal uncle. "Greetings, Uncle."

For a few moments, Sterling just looked at him. "You look wonderful, nephew," he finally said. "Your parents would be proud of you."

Winter honestly didn't know what to reply. He'd been ready for Sterling to rant and rave at him for spoiling his plans, but the older Sidhe had done no such things. Instead, he'd been shockingly helpful, going as far as helping the Cunninghams shield Winter and Corbin of some of the political aspects of the day. For that and for bringing everything they needed for the ceremony, Winter owed him. But that didn't mean he trusted the other Sidhe. For all he knew, Sterling was only using this opportunity to find out more about the Cunninghams so he could later steal Shea.

Even so, the mentioning of his parents touched Winter's heart. "Do you really think so?" he asked in a soft tone.

"I know so." Sterling reached into his pocket and retrieved a pendant in the shape of a teardrop. It was beautiful, and Winter felt immediately drawn to it. "This gem was given to me by your mother to gift on your wedding day."

Winter's eyes widened. "But when? How?"

"The last time I saw her," Sterling replied. "I know you don't trust me, but take this as a present from her, not me."

Winter couldn't refuse such an offer. He knew magic could be deceptive, but this pendant held a piece of his mother. He could just sense her energy, warm and loving. He took the gem and squeezed it in his fist, reveling in the feel of it against his palm. He could almost feel her embrace now, just like when she'd been alive.

"Thank you," he told his uncle. "I don't know how you got this, but thank you."

"My pleasure." Sterling squeezed Winter's shoulder. "I really am happy for you, Winter, and I only wish you the best. Please believe that."

Winter couldn't lie or promise falsehoods, not when he held his mother's pendant in his hand. So he said nothing, even if a small part of him dared to hope his uncle was being honest.

Sterling didn't seem surprised by his silence. "I take my leave now." He started to turn then suddenly stopped. "For the record, I'm proud of you, too."

Without giving Winter a chance to reply, Sterling left the room. Winter watched him go, still wondering about his uncle's change of heart. Then his focus went on the pendant again, and the only thing he could think about was how much he wanted to share this find and this gift with Corbin.

Anxiety and anticipation filled him as he thought about the lynx. Tonight would be their wedding night. He would finally feel Corbin's touch like he'd wanted for so long. Did it matter that the circumstances were far from ideal? Of course not. Whether all these guests knew it or not, the only people who mattered today were Winter and Corbin, and their bond.

With that in mind, Winter resumed his preparations for the ceremony. The pendant went around his neck and under the numerous layers of fabric. Its weight comforted Winter, and for the first time that day, he could honestly say he was absolutely certain he was doing the right thing.

* * * *

"Are you sure this is the place we're supposed to be in?"

Corbin toyed with his cravat, fidgeting in the formal clothes that made him feel out of place. He gave his father an anxious look, hoping the other lynx would have an answer to his questions.

Garth released a sigh of exasperation. "This isn't a human wedding. Hell, it isn't even a shifter wedding. You heard what Winter said. Sidhe are high on ceremony. So since we insisted on holding the wedding here, we have to do everything right."

"Yes, but…The ocean?" Corbin looked down for good measure. Through the transparent platform he was standing on, he could see the fish and other sea creatures swim around. It made absolutely no sense to Corbin that shifters like the Cunninghams had not thought it necessary to wed in the middle of the ocean, even if their inner animal was naturally aligned to the sea, but the Sidhe insisted on it.

"Apparently, their religion demands transcendental coalescence with the Nameless One through the Silver Pool. We're using the ocean as an equivalent."

Corbin knew that. He respected it and had agreed to it. But what made him nervous was that he was here, with his father and most of the guests, whereas Winter was nowhere to be seen. Hell, not even the religious authorities who were meant to bind Corbin and Winter in matrimony had arrived.

There were boats all over the place, as far as the eye could see. Family and friends were close to Corbin in smaller, ornate, almost mystical-looking wooden rowboats. Everyone else was lined up in yachts all around Corbin, while Corbin himself sat on the platform, alone. It was somewhat isolating, and Corbin was thankful he had his family around.

"Don't look so glum," Preston said. "Winter's coming."

Corbin wanted to think that, but with every passing second, it seemed more and more unlikely that Winter could want him. Winter was used to magical platforms forming out of nowhere in the middle of the sea. He'd grown around stoic, insanely beautiful people, and could have anyone he wanted. For his part, Corbin had broken his own share of hearts, but the people he'd been with were all shifters. This was so very different.

"I know he's coming," he told his brother bitingly. "This suit is just uncomfortable."

Preston gave him a knowing look. "Right. Whatever you say, brother."

Layton was just smiling, and when Corbin turned to glare at the seahorse, the younger man directed his full attention to the baby he held in his arms. Shea had been quiet, as if sensing the importance of the moment. At all times, his parents had watched him, mindful not to leave him alone around the Sidhe delegation. But nothing had happened, well, nothing bad. Sterling and his men had minded their own business, simply assisting in the organization of the wedding. It was very confusing.

"I assure you, Winter wants to marry you," Alexis said. "He's just as excited as you are."

The incubus and his mate, Morgan, had arrived a bit later than the other guests, having stayed behind to keep Winter company. As such, Alexis was the last one out of those here who'd seen the Sidhe. Alexis's encouragement meant a lot, but it didn't fully cast aside Corbin's disquiet.

Corbin toyed with his cravat again, this time earning himself a glare from Nicolas. The hummingbird slapped his hand away and said, "Stop it. By the time your mate gets here, you'll make a mess of your clothes."

Corbin might have protested at being treated like a child, but doing so might have pushed Nicolas's boat away from the platform or, worse, cause the hummingbird to fall into the water. In the end, it no longer mattered, as the sound of an approaching aircraft reached his ears. He held his breath, instinctively knowing that finally, the moment he'd been waiting for had arrived.

Silence fell as a small airplane appeared against the horizon. The seconds seemed to drag forever until at last, the plane hovered above the platform where Corbin stood. Corbin wondered how in the world his mate would come to him. He could hardly see a ladder descending from the tiny plane.

The door of the plane opened, and much to Corbin's dismay, several Sidhe stepped out of the aircraft. True enough, the distance between the platform and the plane wasn't very large, but Corbin still hadn't expected it.

The first people who showed up were the Sidhe priests who would be officiating the ceremony. The great prelate always looked like he'd just bitten into a lemon, and today was no different. Winter had told Corbin it was highly unusual for the prelate to leave Sidhe grounds, and the man must probably be in fear for his life. They jumped out of the plane, falling slowly, as if some force was fighting gravity for them. It was quite impressive.

All thoughts of other people vanished, though, when Winter appeared from above. The only word that came to Corbin's mind was *angel*. Winter jumped out of the plane like the priests had. As his mate stepped out of the plane, his majestic motions left no doubt as to his royal blood. His fall was graceful, as if he were a petal that even the planet's force didn't dare to harm.

Winter landed next to Corbin, a smile on his beautiful face. The lining of his clothes seemed to make him glow, and the fall of his crimson hair contrasted with the silver of the outfit. Winter's wedding garb as a whole was not composed out of shirts and pants, but rather robes that were tight against the chest and flared at the bottom. They were almost like Chinese changshans, only with a distinctive magical feel. He was almost too gorgeous, so much so that for a minute, Corbin actually stopped breathing. He couldn't possibly be the one meant to wed this ethereal creature. It was too much of a gift. He didn't deserve it.

"Hello, Corbin," Winter said in a soft voice, and that was enough to snap Corbin out of his trance.

"Hi, sweetheart," Corbin answered. "You look amazing."

And then Winter dropped his outer cloak, and Corbin's mind just about melted. He'd known about the sequence in the ceremony, but merely the swish of the fabric made him want to pounce on Winter. Everything inside him roared to ignore all the guests intruding on their private moment, steal his mate away, and claim him the shifter way.

But this ceremony was important for Winter, so Corbin swallowed his frustration and leashed his beast. Like Winter had taught him, he took his mate's hand and stepped in front of the stoic-looking prelate. Skylar and Byron stood on the side, ready to take heed of the vows.

At last, the Sidhe priest started to speak. Corbin didn't understand quite everything since Winter hadn't actually had the time to teach him the ancient Sidhe tongue. However, for the purpose of the ceremony, Corbin had been provided with a minuscule headset where another Sidhe translated what the prelate was saying.

The translator's voice droned in his ear. "The Nameless One has blessed us all today to witness the union of two souls and two energies. May the blessings of his magic shower over this, your servant, and grant me the power to reach them in his name."

In a way, the words were distracting and somehow didn't suit the way the prelate actually spoke. The ancient Sidhe tongue was a beautiful language, far too beautiful for the translator to fully grasp its flow in English words, and Corbin looked forward to learning it. He could bet it sounded great when Winter was screaming in passion.

Shaking off his lustful thoughts, Corbin focused on the ceremony. Finally, the prelate finished his discourse and the most important moment arrived. Corbin and Winter turned toward each other, entwining their fingers together. Corbin looked straight into Winter's eyes, entranced by the happiness he saw there.

"*K'arian yadar k'adar challa Hastri D'Or orti gar*," they said at the same time. It literally meant, "I vow myself to you under the blessings of the Nameless One."

The words flowed from Corbin's tongue with far more ease than he'd expected. Almost instantly, Corbin felt a power flow over him, foreign but so familiar. It was warm, almost liquid, like the water in a pool lapping against Corbin's skin, and yet electric. Where his hands touched Winter's, it felt like he was touching an outlet. Energy and magic sizzled over his skin, so powerful, but so kind.

Corbin had never been a religious person, but in that moment, he truly sensed there was a higher power watching over them. The prelate's words, beautiful simply through the way they'd sounded, had also been true. And right then and there, Corbin understood that his entire life he'd waited for this. He'd waited for Winter, the only one who could complete him.

Winter released a small gasp, as if overwhelmed by the moment. His smaller hands squeezed Corbin's in a nearly painful grip.

A voice seemed to whisper in Corbin's ear. "Kiss him."

It could have been the translator, or maybe this unseen deity that had blessed their union, but Corbin didn't care. He just knew that he'd never heard of a better idea in his life, well, except the one that had brought them to this point in the first place.

Barely managing to suppress a growl, Corbin pressed his mouth to Winter's. The beautiful Sidhe melted against his chest, his lips parting in a soft, soundless gasp. Corbin greedily thrust his tongue inside the wet cavern, devouring Winter, taking what was his. He hadn't kissed Winter since the day of their rushed engagement, and he was ravenous.

Energy rushed around them, the sound of restless water reaching Corbin's ears. As Corbin broke the kiss to breathe, he saw the entire ocean, as far as the eye could see, sparkled like a white jewel. It was beautiful, almost as beautiful as Winter himself.

In the silence that followed, Corbin distantly registered the shock on the guests' faces. Alexis's eyes were a little glazed, the incubus obviously affected by the lust in the air. The shifters weren't much better off, but Corbin didn't really see anyone except Winter. If he'd looked like an angel before, now…Now, there were simply no words.

When another layer of clothing dropped, Corbin's lynx clawed at his insides, angry at being denied. Winter must have sensed it because he licked his lips, his ice-blue eyes glittering like diamonds. Alas, they were not alone, and nor would they be for a great many hours.

Skylar cleared his throat, notifying them that there were still a couple of formalities to deal with. Normally, shifters would claim their mates in private and register it through the Agency. Now, however, Corbin hadn't actually made the first step since there hadn't been time. The Sidhe bonding ceremony would count as the original shifter claiming, but Skylar still needed to make it official.

Thankfully, the shifters were efficient where paperwork was concerned. A transparent slab emerged from the platform, and Skylar placed the documents on it, not even blinking an eye at the demonstration of magic. After reasserting the fact that they did indeed want to be mates, Corbin and Winter signed the documents. With that, it was finally done. They were married by the standards of both their nations.

Corbin would have expected it to feel more earth shattering, and in a way, it was. However, as he stood there looking at Winter, he realized that, in his heart, he'd been already sworn to Winter. There was just one more thing he needed to do, and he intended to take care of it tonight, after the ceremony.

Confirming Corbin's guess, Winter said, "We should go. Everything is ready for the party back at the house."

Indeed, now that the light on the ocean was starting to dwindle, the ceremony was over. The celebration would be continued at the Cunninghams' household. Knowing that he still had hours to wait before he could feast on the delights of Winter's flesh, Corbin surrendered to the inevitable. He leashed his beast and nodded. "You're right." After a brief pause, he couldn't help but add, "Actually, that house is huge and has many nooks and crannies. Maybe we can lose ourselves in one. The guests will never know."

Winter blushed prettily, the hue of his cheeks almost reaching that of his hair. He looked like he was considering it, but alas, the exchange was overheard. "Don't you dare," Preston said. "You're going to have to stand there and smile like the rest of us did."

It wasn't exactly the same, but Corbin couldn't bring himself to get angry with his brother. In fact, if there was anyone who understood waiting for one's mate, it had to be Preston, who'd been denied his bond for many years. In spite of his animalistic urge to claim Winter, Corbin acknowledged the need for control.

"Don't worry," he told the younger lynx. "We'll behave."

The trip back to the house was uneventful compared to the ceremony itself. Well, in truth, Corbin was too lost in Winter's presence to care about anything else. Unlike before, they flew to their destination in the same aircraft and held hands all throughout the journey. Winter's scent, the warmth of his fingers, and the way he would steal looks at Corbin from time to time, everything was driving Corbin crazy.

By the time they reached the house, Corbin was hard as a rock, painfully so. He felt thankful for the fall of his formal tunic that helped him hide his state. It didn't much help his arousal, but at least no one would be staring at his swollen cock.

Skylar, Byron, Garth, and Nicolas immediately set about to check the last of the arrangements. King Sterling was also in the middle of it all, ensuring his nephew's wedding party went on without a hitch. Corbin still didn't know what to make of the man but decided to worry about it later.

Gradually, the guests began to appear, flooding the house. There were so many people, some of them very important, and Corbin's idea to flee the party early became more and more unlikely.

At one point, Garth approached him, a tall, Asian man following behind him. Corbin had always thought Asian people had a slighter build, but he guessed that the paranormal world was made out of exceptions. And of course, Kaname Yamamoto, the vampire elder with whom Skylar and Byron had been in contact for around a year, could only be one of these exceptions.

Corbin and Winter had met Kaname earlier that day when the vampire had arrived, entourage in tow. Between him, the mer elder, and Sterling, the reunion made for the first time where so many powerful people were gathered together.

"It's an honor to congratulate you on your mating, Tomacelli-san," Kaname said, bowing at Winter. His foreign accent gave the sound of Winter's last name an odd lilt that seemed strangely seductive. Corbin was not amused, especially since Winter's last name was no longer just Tomacelli, but Tomacelli-Mckenna.

Alexis took it all in stride. "Thank you, Yamamoto-san." He offered Kaname a perfect return bow, as if he'd been sharing Japanese greetings all his life. "It is Tomacelli-Mckenna, now."

"Ah, of course." Kaname smiled. "I must apologize. I did not realize you would take your consort's name."

Corbin gritted his teeth in anger but managed to suppress his growl. Of course, he'd known the difference in rank would also be an issue. However, lines needed to be drawn from the very beginning. Winter would be the Sidhe king, yes, but Corbin had no intentions of allowing predators like Kaname to get their grubby paws on Winter.

"I have taken my mate's name in turn," he said. "We're united, you see, and I am convinced that together, Winter and I can achieve many things."

Kaname just arched a brow. "Of course. I admit, you are quite brave to take on the role of a future Sidhe king consort. I admire courage in a man."

Corbin's eyebrows shot up when he realized Kaname was flirting with him, too. A small smile fleeted on the vampire elder's lips, and Corbin's lynx settled down at the realization that the other man was only playing. He didn't actually have any intention of initiating an intrigue or trying to mess with Winter. It was a game, and Corbin started to understand that his life with higher-up politicians would be much like a tennis match.

The ball was in his court now, and Corbin decided it was time to strike back. "Oh, I'm sure that's nothing compared to your initiative to come here, in foreign lands. After all, you don't know the Cunninghams that well."

Kaname chuckled. "You almost sound like you wish I hadn't come."

"Of course not," Corbin answered. "Both Winter and I are honored."

"In fact," Winter added, "we'd love to have you as a guest to the Sidhe palace sometime in the future."

Corbin wrapped an arm around his mate's waist, grinning in contentment. He loved it that Winter had included him in the offer. In fact, it felt natural. As strange as it might have seemed to some that Corbin had become Winter's consort, he actually had experience with meeting important people and solving problems. Perhaps this wouldn't be so hard after all.

Shortly afterward, Kaname took his leave, promising that he would, indeed, take them up on their offer once Winter became king. The mer elder, Kaliad, was here with two sons and one daughter, and it was a wonder to watch them move around, their motions so sinuous and elegant.

But again, there was nothing more beautiful than Winter. As the hours flew by, Corbin was forced to watch as more and more layers fell from Winter's outfit. It was more than Corbin could withstand, and Corbin was amazed at his own resilience when he didn't just abandon all caution and steal his mate.

Several times, Corbin saw something like a shadow of confusion and frustration sweep over Winter, but he couldn't identify the source. He vowed he would ask Winter about it once they got a moment alone.

Still, he could say he was enjoying the anticipation, at least until something unexpected happened. A female figure emerged from the numerous crowd, heading straight toward Corbin and Winter.

Cherise had been one of the many women who'd paraded through Corbin's bed throughout the years. Of course, they'd all known he just slept around and didn't settle down with anyone, so Corbin had never felt guilty about leaving them. Cherise had been different since for some reason, she'd believed she could change him.

Ironically, that wasn't why he'd broken up with her. Cherise had drawn information out of him regarding one of his closest friends. One night, Corbin had gotten drunk, and she'd used it to find out everything about Layton. Corbin had broken up with her after she'd mocked the seahorse with the garnered info.

Corbin was torn between panic and shock. He stole a look at Preston, who, in turn, exchanged glances with Layton. Layton discreetly gestured toward Morgan, and the end result was that Alexis snaked through the crowd and made his way to Winter's side.

"This crowd is such a bother, don't you think?" he asked the Sidhe with a smile. "Join me for a moment while I check up on Elian?"

There was no way Winter would refuse seeing either of the Cunningham babies. He seemed a bit puzzled at the request but acquiesced, regardless. "Sure. It would be my pleasure."

Alexis winked at Corbin over Winter's shoulder, but in the incubus's eyes, Corbin saw concern. So far, his wedding had gone exactly as planned. The important guests had been almost suspiciously well behaved. It would be a pity, and somewhat ridiculous, if Corbin's former squeeze spoiled all the effort.

While Alexis was fleeing with Winter in tow, Isaac and Reed had intercepted Cherise, stopping her from following. Corbin hastily joined them and grabbed the woman's arm. "What are you doing here, Cherise? You weren't invited."

"My cousin was," Cherise replied. "I just took her invitation and decided to crash your little party."

Corbin took a deep breath, cursing himself for ever sleeping with Cherise in the first place. She was beautiful, no doubt about it, but he should have known she would be trouble. "Come with me," he told her, barely managing to keep his anger in check.

Without waiting for her agreement, Corbin started to pull her away from the party. Thankfully, she didn't protest. In fact, Corbin could almost feel her smugness. Perhaps she believed she'd won because he'd gotten Corbin to speak to her in private. Well, that was hardly the case.

Corbin found the first empty room and pushed her inside. Almost instantly, she was on him, her hands greedily pawing at his body. "Oh, baby. I knew you were just excited to see me as I am."

Fuming, Corbin caught her wrists before she could do any damage to his clothing. "What the hell is wrong with you, Cherise? I'm mated. You can't just barge in here and demand I take you back."

Cherise crossed her arms over her ample bosom and scoffed. "And you can't tell me you suddenly fell in love with a man. I know you, Corbin. You're a lady's man, through and through. Your family may be full of faggots, but not you."

Corbin couldn't believe his ears. Prejudice like that was no longer so rampant even among humans, let alone shifters. Shifters had started to understand sexuality wasn't labeled in one way or another, and even if Corbin had actively attempted to pretend to be strictly straight, he'd always been bisexual.

"Just get out of my house," he told Cherise. "Get out before I throw you out."

"You don't mean that." Cherise pouted. "Come on, I get that you're marrying the Sidhe for money. Or political reasons. But the sex? Oh, baby, I'm willing to understand it as long as you share that handsome bod of yours with me."

Corbin felt sick and ashamed that he'd ever even accepted her in his bed. She was tainting this day with her presence. The only good thing was that Winter had not realized it yet, but that could change.

"You insulted my mate and my family," he said between gritted teeth. "I have no idea how you think that will win you any appreciation in my eyes."

Deciding conversation was pointless when people like Cherise were concerned, Corbin grabbed her arm and dragged her out of the room. The important event guaranteed that there were plenty of guards around. They were currently doing their best to avoid looking at Corbin and Cherise, probably thinking exactly what Cherise had. It irked Corbin immensely that anyone would think Corbin would choose Cherise over Winter.

He stopped in front of a guard and pushed Cherise in his arms. "Get rid of her." When the man gave him a befuddled, shocked look, he clarified, "Throw her out and make sure she doesn't get in again."

"Yes, sir," the guard said. "On it."

"You'll regret this, Corbin," Cherise shouted as she was dragged away by several men. "Your little fae won't be able to satisfy you, and then you'll come running back to me."

As the guards disappeared with his nemesis, Corbin sighed and rubbed his eyes tiredly. Things had been going so well, but now, he was in a horrible mood. "Don't mention this to anyone," he told the remaining guards. "I don't want it to spoil Winter's day."

"Yes, sir," the men said as one.

Corbin hoped he could trust them, but he couldn't afford waiting for much longer. He'd already been away from Winter for a long time, and he didn't know how long Alexis could distract the Sidhe.

His concern turned out to be justified. He found his mate waiting for him a few feet from the garden entrance, an expression of heartbreak on his face. Alexis was by the Sidhe's side, looking regretful.

"So it's like that then," the Sidhe said. "All that talk about you feeling something for me was just nonsense, wasn't it?"

Corbin reached for his mate, wincing when the Sidhe pulled away. "Look, it's not what you think," he said, "Cherise is just my ex. She doesn't think I truly have a bond with you. I've set her straight, and she won't bother us again. "

Winter released a bitter laugh, and his eyes were like chips of ice when he glowered at Corbin. "But I notice you didn't deny lying about your feelings. I guess that explains why we didn't bond then."

Corbin gave his mate a look of disbelief. "We are mates," he protested. "Don't deny that."

"My parents used to be able to speak through their minds after the ceremony of bonding was over," Winter shot back. "Why can't we?"

"I still need to claim you by the shifter way." Corbin reached for Winter again. This time, however, he caught the Sidhe, not because he was any quicker, but because Winter allowed it. "Please, sweetheart. Let's just talk. I swear to you I can explain everything."

Winter didn't look convinced. "The guests—"

"Fuck the guests," Corbin interrupted him. "We can go back to the party later. We need this, and you know it."

The beautiful Sidhe nodded. "Okay. You're right. I'll listen."

Feeling a small measure of relief, Corbin smiled at his mate. "Thank you," he breathed out. Turning toward Alexis, he took in the regret in the incubus's eyes with a mixed sense of gratitude and dismay. "It's okay. I got this. Just make sure no one bothers us."

"I'll do my best," Alexis replied. After a brief pause, he added, "You take care, okay?"

Corbin lifted Winter in his arms, making the Sidhe release a protesting squeak. "I will," Corbin told Alexis. "Thanks."

With that, Corbin took his leave of Alexis and headed upstairs toward the room that had been prepared as theirs. He did his best to avoid other folk, but unavoidably, he ran into several guards. He paid no heed to them, even if Winter seemed a touch embarrassed at being seen in this posture. Perhaps it wasn't exactly dignified for a king, and to a certain extent, Corbin regretted it, but Winter couldn't have minded too much as he didn't tried to struggle away from Corbin's grasp.

However, when at last they reached their room, Winter demanded to be released. Corbin obediently set his mate down and waited to see what Winter would say.

"I can't believe you used my friend against me," Winter fumed as he turned to Corbin. "Worse, you run off with your whore during our wedding day? Who the hell do you think you are?"

Corbin stepped in Winter's personal's space and crowded the beautiful Sidhe against the wall. "Alexis knows how I feel about you," he whispered in Winter's ear.

Through his advanced senses, Corbin picked up his sweetheart's arousal. Winter's breath sped up, and his heart started beating faster. Corbin's cock also responded to his mate's proximity, and he felt Winter's own hard prick nudge against his thigh.

"Corbin." His name was a moan on Winter's lips. "God, we shouldn't be doing this. We should talk."

Corbin's hands slithered under Winter's delicate clothing. Even after so many hours, the outfit still had so many layers it was like unwrapping a present. "We're talking, sweetheart," Corbin murmured. "The best way to talk is through our bodies. Then you're gonna know I'm not lying. I've never lied to you."

Winter trembled in his arms, the struggle clear in the beautiful fae's posture. Corbin knew the exact moment when his mate gave up the fight. Winter threw his head back, exposing the pale, white column of his neck in a gesture of pure surrender. The lingering remnants of Corbin's control shattered, and he started pressing kisses to every inch of silky skin he could reach.

Knowing they would still need Winter's clothing for later, he refrained from the urge to simply tear the delicate material off. Instead, he found the clasps embedded in each item for the purpose of easy removal throughout the ceremony. Simply by a press of the twin clasps on each side of the garment, Corbin could get rid of one layer of material that was in his way. It was quite convenient, especially since, even with all the effort he was putting into it, Corbin didn't think he could be patient for much longer.

At last, Corbin reached the last layer, an almost transparent garb that did nothing to cover Winter's gorgeous body and only tantalized with the promise of what lay beneath. Corbin unclasped it as well, and as the material pooled at Winter's feet, he couldn't suppress a groan.

Winter was simply perfect. Corbin didn't know where to look and what to touch first. He was simply enthralled with the beauty and flawlessness of this ethereal being that had somehow become his mate.

But the look on Winter's face was more than real, and the blaze in those ice-blue eyes so intense it almost felt palpable. "Please, Corbin, touch me. Make me believe in you. I want to. I want to so badly."

Corbin took Winter in his arms once again, lifting him up. The Sidhe wrapped his long legs around Corbin's waist, and their lips met in a kiss that was curtained by Winter's mane of crimson hair. Corbin took possession of his mate's mouth, delving deep, branding Winter as his. He simply couldn't get enough of Winter, not now that he finally had the sweet fae in his arms.

His own clothes restricted his options, however, so Corbin walked them to the bed and slowly placed Winter on the mattress. Although he didn't have the same respect for his own clothes as he did for Winter's, he still did his best not to tear them since what little part of him remained rational knew they would have to go back to the party later. Finally, he got naked and joined his beautiful mate on the bed.

As one, they reached for each other, bringing their bodies together in an embrace that had been delayed for too long. Once more, their lips met into a kiss that tasted like need, urgency, and desire. While he thrust his tongue into Winter's mouth, Corbin caressed Winter's flanks, the flame inside him fueled by the simple feel of his mate's silky skin under his fingertips. Winter yielded to his explorations, wrapping his arms around Corbin's neck to pull him even closer.

Their tongues tangled together in a duel that Winter surrendered to. Corbin devoured his mate's mouth, Winter's taste driving him wild.

When they broke apart to breathe, Corbin took a long look at the picture Winter made. His crimson hair was a mess and his face flushed, his lips swollen. Corbin wished he wasn't one person, but two, so that he could touch Winter everywhere at the same time.

As it was, he had to decide, and he started nibbling on Winter's earlobe. Winter thrashed under him, rubbing his naked body against Corbin. He was making needy sounds under his voice, his entire body vibrating with want. "Please, Corb. Please, don't...I need..."

"Shh," Corbin murmured. "I know, sweetheart. I know what you need."

Because Corbin wanted the same thing with a desperate intensity that made even breathing an effort. His cock throbbed painfully, and the only cure for that ache—and for the one in his heart—could be found within Winter's body. Only then would Corbin finally feel complete.

But Corbin had waited too long for this moment to ruin it by rushing. Already, he'd been just one step away from doing just that through that simple conversation with Cherise. Corbin never wanted to have doubts between them again. He yearned to show Winter what their bond meant for him.

All his life, Corbin had been sleeping around without even knowing what he was looking for. He'd told himself that it was all just to have a good time, for both himself and his partner, but in the end, those encounters had left him feeling empty, until finally, they'd made him doubt he would ever find the person meant for him. Now that he had, though, he would not let Winter get away.

He licked down Winter's collarbone, exploring the hollow of the fae's neck with his tongue. Winter gasped and moaned, no longer protesting in the slightest. His voice was a litany of Corbin's name, followed by an ever-present "yes" and "more."

Corbin went lower down, stopping over Winter's plump nipples to suckle on the little nubs of flesh. He'd always had a thing with playing with the teats of his sex partners, whether they be male or female. Some hadn't particularly enjoyed it, but Winter not only liked it. His moans grew louder, more erratic. Corbin's head swam, his half-formed bond with the Sidhe practically teeming with lust.

He lingered for as much as he could take it on the pretty copper disks, and then, when he couldn't withstand the need anymore, he lifted his head and went straight for the gold. Winter's cock, nestled in a small patch of crimson curls, beckoned to him like a beacon. Without a second's hesitation, Corbin took his mate's prick in his mouth all the way into his throat and started to purr.

It was all over in merely instants. No sooner had Corbin started sucking the Sidhe's cock than Winter exploded, filling Corbin's mouth with hot seed. Corbin couldn't say he was taken by surprise. The whole day had been a buildup of sexual tension, and it was a wonder that Corbin didn't come as well merely at tasting his mate's essence.

Seeking the ambrosia of Winter's taste, Corbin drank down all of Winter's offering. He cleaned Winter's already half-hardening cock and looked up at his mate.

"Sorry," Winter said, looking dazed. "I just…I've never…"

God, he was so beautiful Corbin's heart hurt. Corbin released his mate's cock from his mouth, licked his lips, and climbed back over the Sidhe. "It's okay," he said against Winter's lips. "I'm flattered. And we have plenty of time to enjoy ourselves." He paused, arching a brow at his new lover. "Unless, that is, you want to go back to the party. Or talk."

Winter gave him a look of disbelief. "You're joking, right? You're not walking out of this room until you fuck me."

And much to Corbin's surprise, the Sidhe pushed him off, flipping him over until Corbin was on the bottom and Winter on top. The turn of events somewhat surprised Corbin, but it was oh, such a pleasant surprise. Seeing Winter look down at him, his long red hair just barely brushing against Corbin's naked skin, made a new wave of arousal sweep over him.

And then Winter wrapped his small fist around Corbin's engorged prick, and it was Corbin's turn to throw his head back and groan. "Fuck, sweetheart, I'm so close. If you don't stop that, I'm afraid you won't get your wish."

"Oh, I very much doubt that," Winter said wickedly as he moved his hand up and down Corbin's shaft. "I have faith in your stamina."

He rubbed his thumb over the leaking slit, making Corbin's vision blur. "I don't know much about this," the Sidhe admitted, "but I want you to feel as good as I did. I want to taste you like you tasted me."

A bit hesitantly, Winter climbed down Corbin's body. He licked the tip of Corbin's prick experimentally, his little pink tongue gathering the pre-cum copiously leaking from the slit. Corbin almost came on the spot, like Winter had, and bit the inside of his cheek, hoping the slight pain would anchor him.

Then Winter made a tight *O* with his lips and slowly started to take Corbin's prick in his mouth. Corbin clenched his fists in the material of the sheets to prevent himself from fucking his mate's face. He could tell the fae was having trouble adjusting to Corbin's girth. Even so, Winter didn't give up. He relaxed his jaw, taking more of Corbin's cock with every second that passed.

After a while, gagging didn't seem to be a problem for him, and although he didn't quite manage to deep throat Corbin, he was doing a damn good job in making up for his inexperience through sheer enthusiasm. God, Corbin had never felt such pleasure in his life, not even during actual penetrative intercourse. The sensations that assaulted him were incredible, and as his lover began bobbing his head up and down Corbin's cock, keeping his orgasm in check became increasingly difficult.

Finally, Winter did the unthinkable and took the whole of Corbin's cock down his throat. It was too much. With a roar, Corbin came, spending himself in Winter's mouth. But even as he lay there, astonished by the potency of his climax, his prick never really got soft. After all, Winter was right there, naked and oh so beautiful.

Noticing Corbin's interest, Winter grinned. "I told you so, didn't I?"

"That you did, sweetheart," Corbin replied breathlessly. He watched as Winter reached for the nightstand and retrieved a tube of lubricant from inside. Apparently, the people who'd readied the room were well informed as to what Corbin and Winter would need during their wedding night. Right then and there, Corbin couldn't say he minded being catered to.

However, Corbin noticed Winter's hands were trembling as he struggled to open the tube. He remembered Winter was a virgin and got up, stealing the lubricant from his mate as he did so. "Come on, sweetheart," he told Winter. "Let me."

Winter was biting his lower lip as if uncertain. Corbin cupped his face, forcing their eyes to meet. "It's okay, Winter," he said. "We don't have to do anything you don't want to. But I promise, I'll never hurt you."

"I...I believe you," Winter stammered. "I'm just nervous."

Corbin gestured for Winter to climb into his lap. When the fae complied, Corbin opened the bottle of lubricant and poured a liberal amount on his fingers. He pressed butterfly-light kisses to Winter's lips and face as he reached between Winter's ass cheeks to prepare his mate. "Just relax, sweet," he told Winter. "You'll love this."

Slowly, Winter surrendered to the kisses, and Corbin dared to push one finger inside. At first, his mate tensed a little, the invasion obviously surprising him. God, Winter felt so tight around Corbin's finger. How would he feel wrapped around Corbin's cock? Corbin pushed the mind-numbing thought away, focusing on soothing his unsettled mate. He gently pushed the finger in and out, allowing Winter to get used to the sensation and whispering encouragements in the fae's ear. When Winter relaxed, Corbin dared to add another finger.

This time, Winter pushed out, groaning in pleasure. Corbin crooked the digits inside his mate's body, seeking for that spot that would make Winter fly. He knew he'd found it when Winter went rigid and cried out, this time in ecstasy. "Oh, Corbin. Yes! There. Again, please, again! More."

Corbin gave Winter some time to adjust, all the while mercilessly rubbing his mate's prostate. At last, he added a third finger and scissored the digits gently, doing his best to prepare the fae's passage. Corbin's cock was much thicker than even three fingers, and Corbin wanted to avoid his mate's pain at all costs.

By now, however, Winter was completely lost in need. His crimson hair clung to his face and body, humid with sweat, and he was thrusting back against Corbin's fingers, begging and pleading. Corbin couldn't refuse Winter any longer. He pulled his digits out of his lover's body and slicked up his cock instead.

Lying back down, he allowed Winter to remain on top and positioned his cock at Winter's hole. "Bear down on me, sweetheart," he instructed. "Slowly. At your own pace."

With his hands on Winter's hips, Corbin guided his mate, tempering him when Winter would have impaled himself on Corbin's shaft in one single thrust. He watched his lover's face for all signs of discomfort, studiously keeping a leash on the beast within that just wanted to break free and ravage Winter.

They both groaned as Corbin's prick finally breached Winter's body. Only the awe Corbin experienced at watching the play of emotions on Winter's face kept him from turning into a rutting animal. But at last, Winter's body fully engulfed him, the silky heat of his passage gripping his cock in a tight fist.

For a few seconds, Corbin just waited. He knew he was spouting claws, and he couldn't help it, but Winter needed the time to adjust.

And then Winter lifted his body and thrust back down, impaling himself on Corbin's prick.

Corbin snapped. He started thrusting up into his mate while his mate pushed down, crying out every time Corbin hit his prostate. They moved together like they'd been lovers forever, in perfect harmony. It was so carnal, and yet, at a deeply spiritual level, Corbin felt their bodies talking to each other. He felt Winter understand that there would never be anyone else for Corbin, that their bond was forever.

With his mate riding him with such abandon, it was a wonder that Corbin even lasted as long as he did. He blamed it on the previous orgasm that had taken the edge off. But an instinctual urge arose inside Corbin, awakening his every primal instinct. His canines descended, and he pulled Winter down, flipping them on the bed until Winter was on the bottom. His cock never left his mate's body as he bit down on Winter's neck.

Sweet blood flooded his mouth at the same time as his mind was invaded with a rush of thoughts not his own. He thrust one last time inside Winter's passage and came, his climax so powerful it seemed to wipe away his very sense of self. There were no longer any boundaries between his identity and Winter's. Winter's emotions became Corbin's, and Corbin's transferred into his mate. It was a reunion at the most visceral level, and Corbin couldn't believe he'd denied himself and Winter this incredible bond for a year.

All too soon, the haze of pleasure began to dim. Corbin's cock slipped out of Winter's body, and he fell on the bed, exhausted. He managed to muster just enough strength to pull his mate close. As he did so, Winter's voice sounded in his mind. *"You really do love me,"* the Sidhe said.

"I do, sweetheart," Corbin replied in the same way. The awe in his mate's tone spoke volumes about the doubts that had clouded Winter's heart. Corbin couldn't blame his lover, and he was only relieved that their bond had clarified things.

"Oh, Corbin." Winter sighed, cuddling against Corbin's chest. *"You shouldn't let me get away with so many things. I misjudged you, again. I doubted you without even asking."*

"So did I." Corbin kissed Winter's forehead, remembering the time he'd scented sex on Winter and automatically concluded Winter had been fucking someone else. *"But you know, I think I'd have been worried if you hadn't cared. Sure, we still have to work on the trusting each other thing, but we can do it."*

"This bond will certainly help." Corbin felt Winter smile against his skin. *"I was so afraid that what I felt wasn't real, that I was deceiving myself into believing we could have a bond like my parents. But in the end, it came true."*

The happiness coming from Winter enveloped Corbin in a cocoon of warmth and contentment. Corbin realized that he was purring, something he rarely did during or after sex. And now, with Winter, it had happened twice.

Winter chuckled. *"It's cute,"* he said. *"Makes me feel nice."*

Corbin knew what his mate meant. The sweet familiarity and comfort were unlike anything he'd ever experienced before. A shadow intruded on it though, an ache settling over Winter's heart and echoing inside Corbin. "They'd have loved to meet you," Winter whispered out loud. "My parents, that is."

"I'm sure they're watching over us as we speak," Corbin replied. The assassination of Winter's family had affected the beautiful Sidhe greatly. Corbin only hoped that he could help Winter heal, if not forget.

Winter wiped his eyes and released an embarrassed laugh. "I should hope not. I wouldn't want them to see me naked and covered in your spunk."

He looked away from Corbin, squeezing the bright white pendant dangling from his neck. Corbin hugged his back, kissing his nape. "Don't hide from me. You don't have to be strong when I'm around. You can tell me anything."

"I just wish they could have been here to see my wedding day," Winter said as he leaned into Corbin's embrace. "I'm sorry. I spoiled the mood."

Corbin turned his mate around and lifted Winter's chin, forcing their eyes to meet. "No, you didn't, sweetheart. We're mates now, in every way. I want you to tell me everything that's on your mind. Don't be afraid to share it with me." He grinned as his eyes fell on his and Winter's abandoned clothing. "Besides, we should probably clean up and go back to the party. Our friends must be jumping through hoops to keep everyone in check."

Winter heaved a sigh. "I guess. For the record, I'd much rather be here, making love to you." Even as he spoke, he rolled away from Corbin and jumped off the bed.

Corbin licked his lips as he watched his mate's naked ass sway when Winter headed into the bathroom. How could he resist? He followed behind Winter, shutting the bathroom door behind himself. Winter was already starting the shower and turned to look at Corbin. "So you decided to join me, huh?"

"Minx." Corbin swatted Winter's naked ass, thrilled when he saw a little of his cum dribbling from his mate's channel. "Get in there. I want you again."

This was how, a few minutes later, Winter ended up on his knees, sucking Corbin's cock for all he was worth. After that, Corbin took Winter again against the shower walls, the water streaming over them like warm rain, teasing their oversensitized skin. And when it was all over, Corbin could honestly say that for the first time in his life, he felt truly happy.

Alas, their newly discovered bond didn't change the fact that they did, indeed, need to return to the party. Corbin took advantage of the opportunity to dry and comb Winter's beautiful hair. He loved the feel of the silken strands as he caressed them. Several times, he stopped to just inhale his mate's scent, and it was only by miracle that he didn't respond to his lynx's call and take Winter to bed again.

Finally, they got dressed again, fixing their clothing the best way they could when what they really wanted was to take it all off. They left the room and headed downstairs. This time, the knowing looks on the guards' faces held a more congratulatory note, as if they knew exactly just what had transpired. Perhaps they did. Corbin found it impossible to hide how happy he felt as he walked hand in hand with his mate.

They ran into Alexis just as they reached the gardens again. "There you are," the incubus said. "I stalled for as much as I could, but the guests were getting restless."

"Sorry," Corbin said with an unrepentant grin. "We got delayed."

"Well, congratulations for the delay then," Alexis replied. "Come on. You can tell me the details later."

Winter smiled indulgently at his friend, having obviously forgiven the incubus for the earlier trick. It was impossible to get mad at Alexis for anything. The man truly meant well and he wanted everyone to be happy.

As they entered the gardens, however, all the noise and the chatter abruptly stopped. Corbin tried not to feel too self-conscious, but he thought that surely it wasn't all that surprising that newlyweds wanted to spend some time alone. Right?

"We're not just newlyweds," Winter said through their bond. *"We're important figures, and as far as they know, we married for political purposes. They must have jumped to all sorts of harebrained conclusions."*

"Do you regret our little private party?" Corbin asked.

Winter offered him a weak smile. *"Of course not. I'll never regret spending time with you. And now, we should clarify all misunderstandings."*

They found Skylar and Byron in the crowd and made their way toward the Cunningham couple. The two shifters didn't look upset or unsettled in the slightest. Instead, Skylar handed Corbin and Winter flutes of champagne and said, "Our guests are waiting for a toast."

"Of course." Corbin lifted the glass and raised his voice so that everyone could hear. "Thank you all for coming here today to celebrate with us. I apologize for our brief absence." He wrapped an arm around Winter's waist as he spoke. "But I can't be blamed for having such an irresistible mate."

Winter went bright red but didn't protest the words. Instead, he said, "I have been blessed with an amazing mating, and for that reason, I'd like to make a toast. For love and for destiny. For everyone who is here today and for those who couldn't be."

"For all our family and friends who made this possible," Corbin added. "Thank you. We can only wish to all of you that you find the same thing we did."

From somewhere to Corbin's right, a voice that sounded suspiciously like Reed's shouted, "Kiss!"

It was one demand Corbin was happy to comply with. He turned toward his mate and pressed their lips together. Compared to the kisses they'd shared in their bedroom, this one was sedate, almost tame, but it held all the emotion Corbin couldn't contain for the life of him.

When they separated, they were both breathless, their bodies instinctively reaching out for each other. Corbin didn't know what he would have done had a loud cheer not erupted around them, snapping him out of his trance. He managed to look away from Winter's hypnotizing gaze and took in the sight of their guests applauding. Many of them seemed genuinely pleased for Corbin and Winter's happiness. On some faces, Corbin still read skepticism, but as far as he could tell, no one harbored any doubts about the stability of this union.

As they ended the short speech, Skylar and Byron pulled Corbin and Winter away from the crowd. "Byron and I have prepared a little wedding gift for you," Skylar said. "Originally, we wanted to give it to you later tonight, but I think it's better to do it now."

Byron retrieved a set of keys from his pocket and tossed them to Corbin. "This is a key to my personal mansion on a private island," he explained. "Go there. Stay as long as you want. Take some time for yourself. All the arrangements have been made, and I have staff already waiting for you. They're all very discreet and know what to do around a newlywed couple."

"In many ways, we forced this upon you for our own personal reasons," Skylar continued. "Thankfully, you and Corbin are true mates, but our selfishness could have destroyed your lives had it not been so."

"You were right when we talked in the office, Corbin," Byron added. "We disappointed you, and we're sorry."

Corbin was overcome by emotion. He'd never heard Byron Cunningham utter those words to anyone, and it was somewhat humbling that he would do so now.

Winter seemed to realize the importance of the moment as well. "You don't have to apologize, sirs," he told the Cunninghams. "You did so much for me when, by rights, you should have thrown me out from the very beginning. I owe you a lot."

To Corbin's surprise, Skylar embraced Winter. "You don't owe us anything, Winter. You've quickly become a member of our extended family, so you're going to have to accept our peace offer. Go there. Live your love. You deserve it."

Corbin didn't know what to say, so he refrained from making any comments at all. Instead, he wordlessly accepted the offer and shook Byron's hand. After releasing Winter, Skylar hugged him as well, and the clear affection Corbin sensed coming from the seahorse did wonders to heal the rift that had emerged between Corbin and the Cunninghams.

As he broke away from Skylar, his parents approached him, twin smiles on their faces. "Ready to go?" Garth asked.

"Go?" Corbin repeated. When Garth stole a look at the key in Corbin's hand, Corbin gaped. "You can't mean...Now?"

Winter echoed Corbin's disbelief. "We couldn't possibly leave. There are still so many important guests. What will they think?"

"You'll have your whole life to cater to the whims of others," Skylar said. "Believe me, I know. Don't waste these beautiful early days. Just think about yourself and your mate. We'll take care of the rest."

To Corbin's surprise, Winter's uncle appeared out of nowhere and piped up, "I have to agree with Mr. Cunningham. Go. Enjoy your surprise. I'm sure nothing will pop up we can't deal with."

"Will you be staying in LA after the wedding, Uncle?" Winter inquired.

Sterling just smiled enigmatically. "Yes and no. I'll be here for a couple more days, and then I'll make frequent visits. Not to offend our hosts, but I want to see with my own eyes that you're well taken care of. This time, I won't be able to, but I trust your mate will do a much better job than I ever could."

Corbin still didn't trust Sterling, but he figured the Cunninghams could keep the Sidhe king in check. Skylar was right. They did need to be a little selfish, at least now, when they could still afford it.

He shared a look with his mate. "All right," they said at the same time.

"Excellent." Nicolas clapped his hands together. "I took the liberty to have some basic items sent to you there, but you should prepare your personal items. After that, we're ready to go."

Excitement coursed through Corbin as he and his mate rushed back into the house to comply. For a little while at least, they would be free, free to explore their love. If anything could have made this day more perfect, it was this.

And then, just as they reached their room, Winter turned toward him and said, "Corbin, I love you."

Just like that, Corbin felt he'd begun a new life, one of happiness and fulfillment. "I love you, too, sweetheart," he replied. "Now, let's go pack. Our tropical paradise is waiting for us."

Chapter Seven

A few weeks later

Winter knew a lot about islands. As a child, he'd grown up on one. The island where the Seelie Sidhe palace was hidden had countless wards around it and had been deemed invulnerable from outside attacks. Any injuries could be healed at the Silver Pool in the temple. Winter had thought it the ideal place to live. Until his parents had been found dead in their beds, poisoned with a special iron-based substance that was lethal for Sidhe and virtually undetectable in food or drink. The Pool could do many things, but it could not bring people back to life.

After that, Winter had only ever come to his home on his uncle's summons and never visited any other island. But for some reason, when Skylar and Byron Cunningham had made the suggestion, he'd known it was the right thing to do. And he didn't regret coming here one bit.

Winter sighed in contentment as the sun's rays caressed his face. He loved the texture of the sand against his skin and the sound of the waves soothing his senses. He could have just stayed here forever and wallowed in nature's glow. Well, if his mate's presence didn't immediately alert him his day of peaceful relaxation was about to take an interesting turn.

Winter cracked his eyes open and looked up at his mate. Corbin grinned at him and the image flashing through Corbin's mind told Winter what his mate planned. "Oh, no," Winter said, already starting to get up. "We're not doing that again. I love the beach as much as everyone else, but it's not the best place for making love."

It was quite true. Contrarily to the view of all those classical romance novels, fucking on the beach wasn't all that great. Oh, Winter had enjoyed it. He always did when Corbin took him. But after the pleasure was over, it always turned out sand got in the worst possible places.

Corbin reached for him, grabbing Winter before he could get away. "But it's worth it, isn't it?"

Much to his dismay, Winter found that he could not resist his mate's appeal. He melted in Corbin's arms, the lynx's warmth drawing him like a moth to the flame. What had they been talking about? He couldn't remember.

Corbin chuckled and lifted Winter in his arms. "God, sweetheart. You're going to kill me one of these days."

Winter's mate started carrying him back toward the house, but Winter didn't have the patience necessary to wait until they reached their bedroom they shared. "I don't want to wait," he told Corbin. "Let's just stay here."

"I thought you didn't like sex on the beach," Corbin teased as his hands fondled Winter's nipples.

Winter released a small gasp. "That's…That's not fair. You're cheating."

"By what?" Corbin's smirk was pure evil. "Touching you?"

"Yes," Winter exclaimed. "You know I can't think when you touch me."

"So you want me to stop? Is that it?" Corbin sighed and placed Winter down. "Fine. I guess you win. You foiled my plan."

Fuming, Winter tackled his mate. They fell together in the sand, but as soon as Corbin hit the ground, he rolled them over, making Winter end up on the bottom. "Oh, so that's how you want to play it." Corbin's palms traveled over Winter's scantily clad ass, kneading the cheeks gently. "Great idea."

It was the only warning Winter got before his mate ripped off the small shorts Winter was wearing. Without the only item of clothing he wore at the beach, Winter was left completely nude in his mate's arms.

Corbin crushed their mouths together, their mind bond flooded with Corbin's desire and possessiveness. *"You have any idea what it does to me to see you dressed in those things? God, I want to fuck you over and over."*

Yes, Winter did know how much Corbin liked seeing Winter in the tight shorts, which was why he had an endless supply of them. The lynx always ended up tearing them off Winter's body, something Winter not so secretly enjoyed.

Corbin broke their kiss, giving Winter a heated look. "You, my sweet, are a seductive minx." He shot to his feet, grabbed Winter, and draped him over his shoulder like a sack of potatoes. Winter couldn't protest, simply because he got to stare at Corbin's fine ass. The lynx himself only wore a pair of swimming trunks, and Winter made a mental note to remove them as soon as possible.

His mate seemed to have a similar plan. Corbin walked them into the ocean, going just far enough from the shore so that the water reached his waist. There was a smooth rock braving the elements there, where the two of them sometimes came to see the sunrise. It was the type of place Winter had always imagined he'd see merfolk in. Thankfully, the waters around the island were completely safe and clear of all intruders, so Corbin and Winter had complete privacy.

Corbin placed Winter on the rock, and for a few moments, they just stared at the breathtaking scenery. There was no one around but them for miles and miles. The staff at the mansion knew to leave them alone when they were at the beach, and the waters around the island were also privately owned by the Cunninghams. Winter had never felt so complete in his entire life.

Then Corbin pushed off his swimming trunks, leaving them abandoned in the water. Both Winter and Corbin were naked now, in the sun, on the cool rock. Their lips met in a kiss that was as gentle as the lapping of the waves against the stone. It gradually grew more intense, the storm of passion between them releasing as Corbin delved his tongue in Winter's mouth.

Winter crawled onto Corbin's lap, rubbing his ass against Corbin's erection. His anus ached to be filled, and his body was on fire.

"God, sweetheart," Corbin said through their bond, *"I need to have you. I need to be inside you."*

Winter couldn't have come up with a better idea himself. They slipped off the rock and into the water. Corbin broke their kiss and flipped Winter on his belly against the stone. It felt cool against Winter's skin, and the contrast with Corbin's heat behind him, it was just another sensation added to the cocktail of pleasure already brewing inside Winter.

A wet finger rubbed against Winter's hole and slowly pushed inside. It aimed straight for Winter's prostate and rubbed the tiny nub mercilessly, making sparks fly through Winter's body. Winter whimpered, pushing back against the invading digit, seeking more of the penetration.

Corbin was relentless, though. He took his time stretching Winter before he added another finger. Winter knew that, in spite of the animalistic urge to couple they both shared, Corbin also worried whenever they didn't have lube on hand. The lynx was amazingly protective of Winter, and the knowledge that this feeling stemmed from the affection Corbin had for him made Winter relent.

His thoughts began to dim as he surrendered to Corbin's mastery of his body. He heard himself cry out his mate's name, begging and pleading to be fucked, sometimes in the Sidhe language, other times in English. Even those words became slurred and incomprehensible, and over and over, Winter was driven nearly to the edge without quite passing it.

And then Corbin removed his fingers from Winter's body. Winter held his breath in anticipation, expecting Corbin's cock to pierce him now. He knew what Corbin intended just seconds before it actually happened. A raspy tongue swept over Winter's crease, stopping over the tiny entrance. The slick muscle stabbed at his hole like a tiny cock, stretching him and preparing him the way three fingers never could. Every nerve ending in Winter's body was alight, and Winter clung to the rock for all he was worth, trying to find an anchor in a world that quickly started to become surreal.

As Corbin's tongue slipped into his body, Winter went wild. The first time Corbin had eaten his ass, he'd almost refused. He'd thought there was no way Corbin could take pleasure in such an act. But courtesy of their connection, Winter knew Corbin truly enjoyed rimming him. And Winter...Well, who was he to deny his mate his desire?

Whimpering, Winter raked his fingernails over the smooth surface of the rock. He could feel his climax approaching, so very close. He pushed back against Corbin, fucking his mate's face. The sounds Corbin made, low, aroused, and possessive growls, were a palpable caress over Winter's body, teasing his peaked nipples, massaging his prick. In fact, Winter's cock throbbed with the need to come, the ache already gathering in his balls. His lover's talented tongue simply didn't allow him any other option. He just wanted Corbin right there with him.

Obviously hearing this thought, Corbin whispered in his mind, *"Let go, sweetheart. Come for me. I want to hear you scream."*

And Winter did scream. He shouted his pleasure as he came all over the rock, Corbin's voice, his scent, and his touch showering him in pure ecstasy. He felt like the stone beneath him had become a cloud of nirvana, supporting him and caressing him with ethereal fingers.

Just as the haze began to dim, Corbin turned him over, his dark blue eyes gone almost black with passion. Corbin's cock nudged at

Winter's hole, and Winter's body instantly responded, his cock going rock hard again.

He gasped as Corbin entered him, renewed pleasure assaulting his every sense. Water wasn't exactly the best lubricant, but Winter's body was so used to Corbin's prick that he had no trouble taking it. Besides, the previous rimming session and subsequent orgasm had not only prepped him, but they'd also relaxed him. Oh, it still burned, but Corbin took his time in pushing inside, and the ache was not only manageable, but deliciously pleasurable.

At last, Corbin bottomed out inside Winter. Winter clung to his mate's shoulders, choking at the emotion he sensed coming through their bond. In moments such as these, there were no barriers between them, and they were one, body and soul. Winter was always aware of the gift he'd been granted through this connection, but now, more than ever.

Corbin pulled out of him and, in one hard thrust, pushed back inside. As his mate's prick hit his prostate, Winter found himself in a storm of pleasure, sweeping away his very reality. Only Corbin was left, just him and his passion, his love, his heart, bound to Winter's.

Winter thrust back against his lover, and they moved together, seeking the ecstasy of orgasm as one single being. In no time, Winter was close to finding his peak once again. He felt full, his channel stretched to the limit by Corbin's cock, and his soul swamped by Corbin's emotions.

And then Corbin bit down on Winter's neck, claiming him with one bite. Winter's world exploded in a myriad of colors that eventually crystallized into a light so pure it seemed impossible. He came just as Corbin's cock throbbed inside him, releasing hot jets of spunk in Winter's passage. But beyond the physical pleasure of their union, their minds melded together, and in that moment, nothing could separate them. They were two halves of one whole, yin and yang, brought back together by an unexpected, but blessed twist of fate. And Winter loved Corbin so much that he could have died happy if only he had Corbin in his arms.

They floated together for the longest time, lost in each other and in the ecstasy they could only find in their coupling. Corbin's familiar, soft purr made Winter want to throw caution to the wind and stay there forever. But at last, the afterglow began to dim, and Winter discovered the less pleasant consequences of their little sex fest.

His back and ass ached from the abuse they'd suffered. After all, in spite of Winter's creative imagination, a rock was not a soft cloud, or a soft bed, for that matter. But Winter wouldn't have traded the experience for anything in the world. He could easily heal himself, and perhaps he'd actually do so later, but for the moment, he preferred to keep the physical reminder of Corbin's possession.

Corbin pulled him into the water, lovingly cleaning Winter and massaging his sore muscles. Winter leaned against his mate, his knees turning to jelly as Corbin's talented hands worked him.

The lynx kissed his nape and whispered in his ear, "If we don't go now, I'm just going to take you again."

"And what's wrong with that?" Winter shot back.

"Nothing," Corbin answered, "except you deserve being in a bed from time to time."

Winter laughed and pulled away from his mate. He sat on the smooth rock, smiling fondly as he watched Corbin attempt to retrieve the swimming trunks that had drifted away. When at last the errant item of clothing was recovered, the two of them headed back toward the shore.

Usually, when Corbin and Winter came to the beach, they expected Winter's clothes would end up unusable and brought plenty of towels. Alas, this time, Winter had fled on his own, tempting his mate to hunt him. This meant that there were no towels and nothing to cover Winter's nudity. Winter realized this far too late, when Corbin took him in his arms and started the walk back toward the mansion.

"Corbin, everyone will see," he protested. He knew he was a bit of a prude, but he honestly preferred to have Corbin as the only person who looked at him when he was naked.

"It's all right, sweetheart," Corbin said. "The staff knows to stay away except when we call to them. I'd scent them if they were in the area anyway, and I'll go around. Okay?"

Winter trusted Corbin with his life, so he didn't protest further. Instead, he relaxed in his mate's embrace and allowed himself to wallow in the comfortable feeling he always experienced after coupling with Corbin.

As they walked, Winter casually observed the scenery. It was truly a beautiful place, one Winter had learned to love. Beyond the seemingly endless ocean and the white beaches ahead stood Byron's mansion, where Winter and Corbin had been staying for the past few weeks.

Winter had learned the house was quite old, dating back from Byron Cunningham's early years. This was the place where Morgan and Layton had been born, the same day when the existence of the shifters was revealed to the world. Back then, it had been a refuge for the pregnant Skylar. Now, it had become a refuge for Winter and Corbin.

"I wish we could stay here forever," Winter told his mate.

"Well, we might not be able to pull that off," Corbin answered, "but we'll try the next best thing, to remain here as long as we can."

Winter liked that plan, and he couldn't wait to reach their bedroom and show Corbin just how enthusiastic he was about it. Thankfully, Corbin was right and they reached their room without being bothered. Winter was debating between taking a shower—the salt water always made his hair horrible—and going ahead with seducing his mate when a knock sounded at the door.

Confused, Winter shared a look with his mate. "Yes?" Corbin asked.

"I hate to interrupt, sir, but you've received a phone call from Mr. Cunningham," the man on the other side replied. It was the house steward, the person responsible for Corbin and Winter's comfort. "He didn't want us to interrupt your day at the beach, but he said you should contact him as soon as possible."

Arousal and frivolous concerns died out as Winter took in the implications. Byron and Skylar would never have called them had something serious not happened.

Winter pulled on a pair of pants and a shirt, and Corbin did the same thing. "Thank you," Winter told the steward. "We'll do so now."

The steward took his leave while Corbin retrieved his phone. They quickly dialed Byron's private number. Moments later, Skylar's face appeared on the vid connection. His usually composed countenance bore the distinctive marks of stress, and his blond hair was a mess, as if he'd just been running his hand through it.

"What is it?" Winter asked. "What's wrong?"

"It's Shea." Skylar swallowed, the pause a clear sign of agitation in a man Winter had only ever seen calm. "He's sick."

"Sick?" Winter repeated in disbelief. "Why? Since when?"

"He's been moody and crying for a while now, but we didn't think anything was wrong. Alexis felt it first, and we had doctors see him. It doesn't seem serious, but no one knows what's wrong." Skylar sighed. "I'm just...I have a bad feeling, Winter. I know I shouldn't bother you on a hunch, but you're a healer. You can help my grandson, I just know it."

"We'll be home as soon as possible," Winter replied. The words fell off his lips with striking ease, and he realized that he had indeed come to care about the Cunninghams as if they were his own family.

"Thank you," Skylar replied, obviously looking relieved. "We'll be waiting."

Winter ended the connection, aware of the importance of each second. They didn't even bother to gather their belongings. Winter just grabbed his mother's pendant from the drawer and rushed out, Corbin hot on his heels.

The steward met them in the foyer. "I took the liberty to ready a helicopter for you. It's outside, waiting."

Winter briefly thanked the man and followed his lead to the helipad. As he and Corbin got inside the aircraft and buckled in, Corbin inquired, "Do you really think Shea's disease isn't serious?"

"I won't know until I see him, of course," Winter replied, "but somehow I doubt Skylar is the alarmist type. He wouldn't have called without good reason."

"What gets me is that sicknesses don't stick to us shifters. What could possibly be wrong?"

There were many things that could go wrong for children. The genetic implications of the reproduction of half-breeds like Morgan and Layton could be, on their own, a concern. But Winter knew that Skylar and Byron had anticipated such issues and had the best staff money could buy ready for their sons. So what could be wrong?

Winter had always thought Elian was more at risk to develop some sort of disease as a child between a shifter and a magical creature. As much as he'd have wanted a baby with Corbin, he was thankful that gift had been lost a long time ago. He didn't want to make the same mistake others had.

"Do you truly think that?" Corbin whispered in his mind, having obviously caught onto the thought. *"Do you think our mating and theirs was a mistake?"*

"No, of course not," Winter replied hastily. *"It's just...From a medical perspective, it's risky for the children."*

"I know," Corbin replied. *"Remember Isaac, Brody and Soren's brother? He had a lot of problems growing up. But that doesn't make his parents' mating wrong or his birth a mistake."*

Winter winced. He knew how standoffish he must have seemed to Corbin. *"It's not like that. I love the children, you know I do. I'm just worried."*

Worried that Shea would die, like Winter's parents had. Worried that once again, Winter would be too late to save a person he cared about. What use did he have for his powers if they couldn't rescue the people who were important to him?

Wordlessly, Corbin gathered him close. Winter buried his face in Corbin's chest, trying to soak in his mate's strength. He had a feeling he would need it.

* * * *

"And we need to look into the replacement of Elder Mercier, Majesty. Paris needs a new leader."

Sterling extended his hand at his assistant. "Files for potential candidates?"

The younger Sidhe handed him a thick folder, already well aware of Sterling's preference to read on paper. "I also sent the file to your computer, Majesty."

"Very good." Sterling paused and gazed at his assistant. "Now tell me, how are things going in my absence? I trust everything has been run according to my instructions."

"Of course, Majesty," the other man replied. "We live to serve."

Sterling had doubts about that. His brother and Jayna had been killed because of traitors in the palace. Now, Sterling had to divide his time between watching over Shea Cunningham and official Sidhe business. He was vulnerable, and he knew it. But he didn't have a choice. The Oracle had told him Shea was the key to keeping Winter alive. Sterling had to delegate at least some of the issues, or else he'd never have the time to make sure Winter's future was secure. At the same time, he found that he cared about Shea. He'd briefly met Layton and Preston's son at the wedding, and even if he hadn't spent too much time around the child, he'd felt a warm pull toward Shea, a protectiveness he'd only ever experienced toward Winter, and yet, somewhat different.

Sterling shook himself, deciding to put aside his own conflicting emotions for the moment. He opened his mouth, intending to ask his assistant about the grand prelate. The prelate had seemed a bit too mouthy and questioned Sterling's orders. The words never came. A piercing sensation at the back of his skull notified him something was very wrong.

"Go," he barked at the younger Sidhe instead. "I wish to be alone."

His assistant took off with a frightened look on his face, but Sterling didn't have time to worry about that. As soon as he was alone, he locked the door and turned around. Just like he expected, the Oracle manifested in front of his very eyes.

"What's wrong, Great One?" Sterling asked. "Is it Winter?"

"It's Shea," the Oracle replied. "It has begun."

Sterling gaped at her. "But I was just in LA yesterday," Sterling said. "Shea was fine."

"And he still is, in a way. You can still stop it. The veil has been lifted off my eyes." The Oracle's blind gaze fixed on Sterling's face. "Shea bears a terrible burden, Sterling. The shadow of the spell on his birth father will kill him."

In one single moment, comprehension dawned. Of course. Spells like the one on Layton Cunningham didn't just disappear without a trace. They left remnants behind. If the people in question were lucky, those traces eventually vanished in time. But in rare cases, that lingering power could cling to loved ones of the original enchanted person, particularly offspring.

Had Sterling brought Shea here, the baby would have been safe from any curse. The wards around the Sidhe island would have obliterated the spell's shadow. It was still not too late. He could steal Shea and bring him here.

"That won't work," the Oracle told him. "The spell was formed with the help of an incubus. Tearing the child away from his parents in a violent manner would just worsen his condition. Had Winter complied with our request, it would have worked out. The shadow still hadn't manifested fully, and Shea cares about Winter. But that is no longer a path we can take."

"Then what must I do, Great One?" Sterling asked. He was beginning to understand where Winter fit into all this, and he didn't like it.

"Listen closely and do exactly as I say," the Oracle replied. "We still have a chance to help Winter and Shea if we do things right. Now hurry. You have to make a pit stop on the way, and there's not much time."

Chapter Eight

The trip back to the Cunningham mansion seemed to take ages, with Corbin worrying about both his nephew and his mate. Winter was fretting, his mind a jumble of confusing ideas Corbin couldn't make heads or tails of. Some of those thoughts upset Corbin greatly, for purely selfish reasons. This was honestly not the time to worry about why Winter wouldn't want a child with him.

Still, Corbin held his mate tightly all the way back to LA, almost thinking that he'd lose himself in his own dark musings if he didn't do so. He only released Winter when the helicopter landed and the pilot told them it was okay to get out.

Corbin opened the helicopter door, and both he and Winter jumped out. Corbin's parents, together with Skylar Cunningham, were waiting for them. Garth's face was guarded, while Nicolas and Skylar seemed concerned.

"Take me to see Shea," Winter said without preamble.

As they walked, Garth started to explain the child's condition. "He was never really sociable, but it's gotten worse. He doesn't stand for anyone except his parents to approach, and when they leave, he doesn't eat, refuses all care, and even gets physically ill."

"When I called, he'd just had a high fever, all because Layton had gone to lie down after forty-eight hours with him," Skylar said. "He was in the next room, Winter, and Preston never once left Shea's side. And yet the fever didn't stop until an hour after Layton returned to hold him."

Corbin couldn't figure out what kind of disease could cause symptoms like those described. "So, it's emotional dependency? Could it be psychosomatic?"

"Doctors are studying the possibility, but they can't give a one hundred percent certain diagnosis," Nicolas replied. "Winter, can you find out?"

"I will try," Winter answered. "Thank you for trusting me with this. I will do my best to help Shea."

They stopped in front of the nursery Shea and Elian used to share. "We moved Elian to a room adjoining his parents'. He and Shea got along great in the beginning, but lately, Shea couldn't even stand his presence."

That was very strange, indeed. Skylar knocked at the door gently, and a few seconds later, a haggard-looking Preston opened it. He offered Corbin a weak smile. "Hey, brother. Sorry about interrupting your honeymoon."

"Don't worry about it," Corbin replied automatically. "How's Shea?"

"He's sleeping right now," Preston murmured. "Come on in. Be careful. We don't want to wake him."

"We'll stay outside," Garth said. "We don't want to disturb him."

Wordlessly, Winter and Corbin slipped inside the room and closed the door behind themselves. The nursery was quiet and quite dark. The sunlight barely filtered through the thick curtains shielding the windows. Through his feline vision, Corbin spotted a small figure on the couch. It was Layton, holding his son to his chest.

As soon as Corbin and Winter approached the couch, Shea opened his eyes and instantly started to cry. Layton shushed him, whispering soft endearments to his baby. When Preston sat down next to Layton, Shea began to calm down, but he never quite stopped crying.

"Can you help us, Winter?" Layton asked, his voice broken. "Please. Something's wrong with him, and no one can tell us what."

Corbin's heart hurt. He couldn't stand seeing his brother, Layton, and Shea suffer like this, and he knew Winter felt the same. The Sidhe knelt next to the couch and reached for Shea. Without removing the baby from his birth father's arms, Winter lowered his hands over Shea's small face. Corbin watched as Winter's eyes closed and his palms started to glow. Everyone was completely silent, the hope and breathless anticipation in the air obvious.

Then, much to Corbin's horror, Winter's complexion grew pasty. He started to choke and sweat, his crimson hair clinging to his face in wet clumps. Corbin sensed a darkness struggling against Winter, lashing out at him from inside Shea. Terrified, Corbin reached for his mate, intending to snap Winter out of his trance. Something stopped him from doing so, a knowledge that Winter could handle this. *"Give me a moment,"* Winter whispered in his mind. *"I can handle this."*

And, indeed, Shea's color began to improve and his cries quieted down. Finally, the glow on Winter's hands diminished. Winter fell back against Corbin, panting hard.

A few seconds passed while Winter recovered. Finally, Winter struggled to his feet. Corbin helped his mate as much as he could, the fright he'd gone through still very present in his mind.

"I have some good news and some bad news," Winter told Preston and Layton. "Which one do you want first?"

"Just tell us already," Preston replied. "The bad news."

A part of Corbin already knew what Winter was going to say. He didn't quite understand it, but he was still unsurprised when Winter said, "Your son suffers from something we call the shadow of a curse. After a spell is broken, lingering traces remain behind. Sometimes, they can attach themselves to the close ones of the originally cursed person, particularly offspring, who are, by nature, vulnerable."

Corbin hadn't thought Layton could get any paler, but he did. "So, it's my fault. My God...I should have known that spell couldn't go away just like that. I should have realized..."

"It's not your fault," Winter interrupted Layton. "None of us realized it, not even me. Shadows are many times latent and undetectable until they actually manifest. You couldn't have known."

Layton's lower lip trembled, and he looked a step away from crying. In Corbin's experience, Layton never cried, but of course, in these circumstances, all bets were off.

"Can you heal it?" Preston inquired.

"Not by myself," Winter answered. "Magical afflictions are more potent than usual ones, and when there's only one healer involved, there's a chance for the curse to fight back strongly and recoil against both healer and patient." Winter paused and licked his lips. "But if I were to take Shea to the Sidhe palace, the island wards alone would shatter the curse, and the Silver Pool could deal with any possible trace it might have."

Layton tensed visibly. "You want to take Shea?" He gave Winter a suspicious look. "No. I can't trust you."

"Your uncle wanted to kidnap him before." Preston narrowed his eyes at Winter. "How do we know this isn't some sort of trick?"

But it wasn't, and Corbin knew very well that Winter was telling the truth. "Calm down. We're all family here, and we want what's best for Shea."

"Look, I understand your point," Winter said, "and I know that it does seem very suspicious. If you're willing, I can discuss it with my uncle. Perhaps we can find some middle ground, so that Shea doesn't have to be transported there. Maybe we could bring more healers, and together, we should be able to deal with it."

"Will that work?" Layton asked. "Will it be enough?"

Winter nodded. "Yes. The shadow curse has just awoken, and it's not as virulent as it could be. For now, Shea is safe, as I managed to leash it. But he must be kept away from anything that could trigger a worsening of his situation. He needs to be kept happy and calm at all times. Family should visit him, but preferably one at a time, so that he isn't overwhelmed. I will try to contact my uncle and arrange for other healers to come."

Preston squeezed his mate's hand and shared a look with Layton. "We should know…What's the worst thing that could happen?"

Winter grimaced, and Corbin saw the images and information in his mate's mind. He wanted to tell Preston not to pursue it, that at least Layton should be spared the torture and the fear. But he saw the decision in both men and knew he could not change their mind.

After a moment of hesitation, Winter slowly started to explain, "The spell on Layton had three parts. One affecting the body, another affecting the mind, and the third one affecting the soul. Right now, only the third one is active. It was the weakest, as your mate bond took care of most of it. But should the other two come out of latency, Shea could become very sick. For Layton, the corporal component referred to lust, but Shea's age means he cannot experience sexuality. Therefore, there are chances that it might transfer into something else, most likely physical pain. The same thing could happen for the mental side of it. But again, I can't be certain, as shadow curses are very varied and complex."

Layton took a deep breath, as if bracing himself. "Very well. Thank you for telling us."

Winter simply nodded and took Corbin's hand. "We'll go contact my uncle now. If there are any developments, if Shea's condition worsens, call me right away, all right?"

After being reassured that they would be notified should there be any change in Shea's state, Corbin and Winter left Shea alone with his parents. They headed out to their room, walking in silence, lost in thought.

"I'm sorry about earlier," Winter finally said. "I hurt you through my selfishness. Again."

Corbin pushed the door to their room open. "It's not that I don't understand, sweetheart. I do. But I'd still like to have a family with you, if it were possible."

At Winter's remorseful look, Corbin decided now was not the time or the place to discuss such things. His mate was tired, the healing process having taken a lot out of him. "Let's leave it for now. After all, you're not a seahorse like Layton. You couldn't give birth to a child if you wanted to."

Winter nodded, but an expression of regret crossed his face. He plopped onto the bed and offered Corbin a small smile. "I'll get some shut-eye. Wake me if there's any problem with Shea."

Corbin lay down next to his mate and watched as the beautiful Sidhe surrendered to slumber. There was so much still separating them in spite of both their efforts. But Corbin swore that he'd get Winter to see that, with enough love, any obstacle could be surpassed. He only hoped this would apply for Shea's curse as well.

* * * *

Winter opened his eyes to a distinct feeling of wrongness. He distinctly remembered falling asleep at Corbin's side, but now, his lynx mate was nowhere to be seen. *"Corbin?"* he asked through their bond.

"Hey, sweetheart," Corbin answered. *"Sorry I couldn't be there when you woke up. Wait for me there, okay?"*

"Why?" Winter inquired, instantly alarmed. *"What's wrong?"*

The question was somewhat rhetorical since through their bond, he could see and hear Corbin's thought processes. Anger and frustration coursed through him as he got his answer. *"Your ex? She's here?"*

"Apparently, she got wind of our return and she wants to stir some trouble," Corbin replied. *"Don't worry about it. We're politely ushering her out because we don't want any fuss with Shea in a delicate condition."*

Winter agreed with those precautions, but at the same time, he wanted her out of Corbin's proximity as soon as possible. More information trickled in his mind, and he understood that he couldn't just stay put as Corbin seemed to want. He needed to make a stand.

As quickly as possible, he found some clothes and changed from his sleep-wrinkled outfit. He combed his long hair and tied it back, then rushed outside, following his instincts to guide him to his mate. He found Corbin in the office with his parents and the same woman Winter had briefly caught sight of at the wedding. There were two other people there, a man and a woman, grouped around Corbin's ex.

"There's nothing for you here," Winter said without preamble. "Leave and don't come back."

The woman narrowed her eyes at Winter. "Who do you think you are, you little faggot? Corbin's my mate. Mine. He promised me he would mate me. I'm pregnant with his child. I won't allow your interference to push my baby into growing up fatherless."

Winter froze. According to Corbin, he hadn't been with his ex in over a year, since before he'd met Winter. If what she said was true, Corbin had deliberately deceived him. Would it be so hard to believe? After all, Corbin wanted a family. Their earlier debate clearly illustrated that.

Winter shook himself, cursing his own lack of trust in his mate. "Go spout your lies someplace else," he told her. "If you are pregnant, that child's not Corbin's."

"I'm afraid it's his word against hers," the woman with Corbin's ex said. "And I'm inclined to believe my daughter. We might not be very traditionalistic, but the least Cherise deserves is some compensation for her suffering and humiliation."

"With all due respect, Madam," Corbin said, "whatever suffering she experienced at my hands is hardly worthy of compensation. We were never lovers, and I haven't touched her in over a year." Corbin wrapped an arm around Winter's waist. "Like Winter said, if she is pregnant, the child is not mine."

Cherise's parents must have actually believed their daughter because they seemed furious. Garth intervened before the situation could worsen. "You've exposed your points, Cherise, and so has Corbin. There's no reason for you to stay here any longer. If you do insist that Corbin is the father of your child, the solution is easy enough. We'll schedule a DNA test as soon as possible. For now, I'm going to have to ask you to leave."

For a few seconds, it seemed like Cherise and her parents would agree to Garth's command. But then the unexpected happened. Out of nowhere, Cherise retrieved a gun and pointed it straight at Winter. "I will have you dead for this."

Several things went through Winter's mind. He wasn't afraid, as, in general, Sidhe weren't particularly vulnerable to normal lead bullets. Cherise was unlikely to know about Sidhe vulnerability to iron, so she probably wouldn't have thought of bringing special ammo. Furthermore, the weapon was very small, tiny really, its small size doubtlessly the reason why she'd managed to sneak it past the Cunninghams' guards. However, a bullet that caliber could hardly cause too much damage in a shifter or a Sidhe.

"Please, Cherise," Garth said, "put the weapon down before you hurt yourself or someone else."

Cherise suddenly gained a hunted look. "No. I won't lose, not to someone like him."

Suddenly, Nicolas, who had been quiet until then, produced a small knife and threw it at Cherise. The weapon flew and unerringly embedded itself in Cherise's arm. She dropped the gun with a cry and fell to her knees.

Chaos erupted as Cherise's parents tried to reach for her. Preston and Skylar burst into the office, followed by several guards, while Cherise scampered for the gun.

Foolishly, Cherise's family tried to block any attempt of others to capture her. While they couldn't take the larger number of people intent on Cherise's immobilization, their intervention allowed Cherise the delay she needed to grab her weapon again.

She directed her gun at Winter and, without hesitation, pressed the trigger. Seconds later, pain exploded in Winter's shoulder, and he realized he had been mistaken. She did indeed know about Sidhe vulnerability to iron, as was proven by the iron bullet currently lodged in his flesh.

Corbin released a roar of anguish and caught Winter before he could fall to the floor. In the meantime, Winter was distantly aware of Preston approaching Cherise and reaching for the gun. Probably in a fit of insanity, Cherise pointed the weapon at Preston and shot.

It could have ended much worse, but thankfully, the bullet just grazed Preston without causing significant injury. Much to Winter's relief, Preston subdued her with ease. Winter could focus on his own problem and eliminate the iron from his body.

Gritting his teeth, he clutched Corbin's arm and centered his energies on the foreign object lodged in his flesh. Mentally, he pushed the bullet out of him. He heard it fall to the floor with a silent thud, and immediately felt a weight come off his chest as the poison started to clear out of his bloodstream.

By the time the healing process was over, he was left as weak as a pup and ready to sleep for a week. Corbin lifted him in his arms just as Byron Cunningham stalked into the office.

"I can't believe this insanity." Byron growled. "You two, get out of my house," he told Cherise's parents. "Your daughter stays here, and she won't see the light of day until I say so."

The two shifters tried to protest, but the guards were already obeying his orders and removing the intruders. Winter was greatly relieved, and he hoped his mate could take him back to their room now.

It was not to be. Skylar burst into the office, an alarmed expression on his face. "Shea! Shea's seizing. Come quick."

Still carrying Winter, Corbin ran after Skylar, who led them and their friends into the nursery. There, a desperate-looking Layton watched as doctors forced Shea into medical equipment meant to help him breathe.

The situation didn't look good. The child's vital signs were poor, and he was making whimpering and wheezing sounds. It didn't take a genius to figure out what had happened. Because of the shoot-out below, the spell had awoken. There was nothing the doctors could do to help Shea.

Quite honestly, Winter didn't know if he had it in him to save Shea, either. Even in normal circumstances, Winter wouldn't have been able to fight a shadow curse on his own. His healing powers were great courtesy of his royal ancestry, but he was still young and this particular spell complex. To make things worse, the bullet wound had weakened him and drained him of energy.

Regardless of this, Winter knew he had to try. He couldn't just let the baby die. He gestured for Corbin to put him down, and the lynx reluctantly did so.

"Sweetheart, you're not well," Corbin said. "Please be careful."

Winter kissed Corbin on the cheek. "I will. I promise."

Gathering his strength, Winter approached Shea's bed. The doctors let him pass, and Winter cleared his mind as he took Shea's tiny hand in his own. Instantly, the spell struck him, with such force that for a few moments, Winter himself couldn't breathe. He sought the power of his bond with Corbin and turned it into healing energy, fighting back against the hostile magic.

At first, it seemed like it would work. The shadow spell retreated in front of Winter's energies. But just when Winter thought he'd won, another wave of dark power assaulted him. Already weak, Winter could not hold it at bay. It shattered his every barrier, and pain wreaked havoc over Winter's mind and body as the spell reached his very core, polluting his magic.

With his final strength, Winter called out Corbin's name, trying to express everything that had remained unsaid between them. He didn't get the chance, and his world turned into darkness and void.

* * * *

Corbin sat by his mate's side, blankly staring at the screens that monitored Winter's condition. His sweetheart lay on the hospital bed, looking so still and so pale. The fall of his crimson hair made his complexion seem even more ghastly. The hand Corbin held in his own felt far too cool and limp. It was hard to believe that mere hours before, they'd been happily making love on the private island.

After healing Shea, Winter had fallen into a deep coma and doctors weren't giving him many chances of survival. Worse still, Winter's connection with Corbin seemed frayed and was getting weaker by the moment. Even if Corbin wasn't inclined to trust the medics, he trusted his bond with his mate.

Distantly, Corbin heard the door open. "How is he?" Preston asked in a soft whisper.

"Bad. Getting worse. I tried to reach his uncle but didn't get any answer."

He'd called King Sterling with the hope that the Sidhe royal could do something to heal Winter. If Winter was right about the Silver Pool on his home island, Corbin guessed that it could very likely help Winter as well. But Sterling was nowhere to be found, and the assistant he'd managed to contact said he'd unexpectedly left without giving any explanations. Upon hearing Corbin's urgency, the Sidhe had promised to continue trying to reach the king. However, Corbin feared that by the time it happened, Winter would be beyond aid.

Preston squeezed Corbin's shoulder. "I'm so sorry. This is my fault. Had I not been grazed by the bullet, Shea wouldn't have needed Winter's assistance."

Corbin shook his head. He was the only one to blame, for not being able to get rid of Cherise before Winter got involved, before she became violent. He'd been a fool to attempt reasoning with her, and now, he was paying the price. "It's not your fault," he said. "It's mine." He took a deep breath and struggled for composure. "How's Shea?"

"Better," Preston answered. "He's sleeping, although I expect he might need further treatment."

At least Winter's sacrifice hadn't been for naught. It might not make Corbin feel any better, but a small part of him managed to be happy for his brother. The rest was all pain, loss, and grief. If Winter died, Corbin didn't think he would survive.

Preston said something else, but Corbin didn't hear it. He was watching his mate's face and chest, expecting that any moment now, his mate would stop breathing. He was so focused on it that the sudden opening of the door startled him.

He turned, ready to attack whoever had dared to interrupt Winter's rest. The last thing he expected was to see Sterling Tomacelli standing in the doorway together with someone Corbin didn't know.

Sterling approached the bed, eyeing Winter with obvious relief. "Thank the Nameless One. We're not too late."

"Do you know how to help him?" Corbin immediately asked.

"Yes." The king nodded. "We need a large body of water. A tub would do if nothing else is available, although it would be preferable for it to provide more space."

"The Cunninghams own a huge pool," Preston offered. "I'm sure they wouldn't mind it if we used it." He pointed at the stranger. "But what's he doing here?"

"He's here to help." Upon noticing Corbin's confusion, the king explained, "This is Chantay, Rhys Whitaker's half brother. There's no time to explain. You're just going to have to trust me if you want to save your mate's life."

Corbin didn't trust Sterling, but no one except the Sidhe could know how to help Winter. "Just tell me what to do."

"The most important thing is to never let go of Winter. The backlash from the spell should have killed him, and it probably would have, but your bond is keeping him alive."

The knowledge of how close to death Winter was made Corbin's head spin. "Okay. I can do that. What else?"

"Grab him and lead the way to the pool. We need to make haste."

With as much gentleness as he could muster in the circumstances, Corbin took his mate in his arms and followed behind Preston as his brother directed them to the pool. Sterling and Chantay came after them. In the hallway, a group of quiet Sidhe waited and joined Sterling at one sign from the king. Skylar was with them and followed as well, looking worried and confused.

But none of them mattered, no one except Winter. Corbin focused on his bond with his mate, fueling it with all the love he felt for the Sidhe. At last, they reached their destination, the huge pool Byron had built for himself and his family.

"All right," Sterling said. "Go into the water with him. It would be better if you were undressed, but we don't have the time to disrobe. You, too, Chantay."

Corbin obeyed Sterling's instructions to the letter. He stepped into the water, still holding his very pale mate, with Chantay trailing behind him. As he moved, the rest of the Sidhe with Sterling surrounded the pool from all directions.

Sterling retrieved a vial of a strange-looking liquid and poured it into the water. "This magic comes from the Silver Pool," he explained. "Normally, no one is allowed to remove even one single drop from the island, but exceptions are made when the life of a member of the royal family is in jeopardy. Now, take Chantay's hand and focus on your connection with Winter. Close your eyes and relax."

Corbin did as he was told and reached out to Winter with every fiber of his being. Chanting started around him in the same language that had been used at his wedding with the Sidhe. And just like then, Corbin felt a welcome warmth envelop him, the presence of a being more powerful than him supporting him and guiding his actions. He flooded their connection with every emotion in his heart. *I love you, Winter. Come back to me, sweetheart.*

All of a sudden, their mate bond was flooded with something Corbin could only describe as darkness. He gritted his teeth, and it roared through him, thousands of needles slashing at his mind and his spirit.

But there was someone else there with him, another mind and another body that had nothing to do with Corbin's bond with Winter. Just when Corbin thought he would lose this battle, that person stepped in, braving the spell.

And then the comfort of the strange presence surrounded them all, and the pain melted into contentment. Corbin opened his eyes, unsure as to what had happened.

"Corbin?" a weak voice inquired. "What's going on?"

At first, Corbin almost thought his eyes were deceiving him. Still in his arms, Winter now looked so much better. The pallor had been replaced by a healthy glow, and while his eyes looked dazed, the sickness had clearly left him. For his part, Corbin didn't feel too affected by the spell's attack.

On the other hand, Chantay had gone gray, much like Winter had been the first time he'd braved the shadow curse. The water was glowing softly, seeming almost fluorescent, and the light emanating from it made Chantay seem almost ghostly.

Several other Sidhe entered the pool and helped the three of them out. "What just happened?" Corbin asked Sterling.

"We used an ancient Sidhe incantation to exorcise the spell. However, the shadow curse was very strong and couldn't be wiped out completely. There was a risk that it might strike back. In fact, it was likely that, because of your bond with Winter, it would loom over you."

"I'd have gladly done it," Corbin protested.

"I know," Sterling answered. "But if something happened to you, Winter would have never survived it, and that would have defeated the purpose of the entire process. As such, we had to pool the remnants into Chantay."

Corbin looked at Chantay, struck dumb by the extent of the sacrifice. "It was the least I could do," Chantay said softly. "After all, my father was the one who helped create it in the first place, and since I'm half-incubus, half-Sidhe, I can withstand the magic better than most."

At last, Corbin remembered his brother had once upon a time mentioned meeting Rhys Whitaker's half brother on his birth father's side. At that time, Corbin had remained behind to take care of the Agency in the absence of his fathers and the Cunninghams. He'd been so lost in his pain over his mate's condition that he'd completely forgotten about it.

Winter, however, seemed to know Chantay. "It wasn't your fault, Chantay," he said. "Children shouldn't have to pay for their parents' sins."

But Chantay didn't look sad or regretful in the slightest. He bowed lowly in front of Winter. "Your words honor me, Your Highness. I consider it a privilege that His Majesty trusted me with such an important task in spite of my father's deeds."

Winter still seemed worried. "Uncle, I'd like you to take Chantay to the island and shatter what's left of the spell. I won't have him suffer in the slightest."

"Of course, Winter." Sterling smiled, and to Corbin's surprise, he looked genuinely happy. "Don't worry about a thing. I have it all figured out."

Suddenly, Winter's eyes widened, and he started to panic. "What about Shea? What happened to him?"

"He's fine for now, sweetheart," Corbin replied. "You saved his life."

"I'll make arrangements with his parents to take him to the island, too," Sterling added. "Even if they don't trust me, we'll come up with some sort of compromise. You took most of the curse upon yourself when you healed him, so he's safe."

It occurred to Corbin that he had no idea how Sterling even knew about Shea. In fact, the entire ceremony that had brought Winter back from death's door had been very complex. There was no way Sterling could have just guessed what was needed.

Obviously realizing this as well, Winter gazed straight at his uncle. "You knew. You knew about this."

"Not until earlier today, at least not in detail," Sterling replied. "It's why I insisted on bringing Shea to the island. Had you obeyed me then, none of this would have ever happened."

"But, Uncle, how was I to know?" Winter asked. "Why didn't you say anything?"

"Would you have believed me?" Sterling waved a hand dismissively. "It doesn't matter anymore. The important thing is that you're safe, and Shea and Chantay will be healed."

Corbin could tell his mate wanted to question Sterling further, but Winter was clearly too tired. *"Later, sweetheart,"* Corbin told the young Sidhe. *"For now, you need to recuperate before you worry about anything else."*

"Okay, Corbin." Winter dropped his head on Corbin's shoulder. *"And...I love you, too."*

At first, Corbin didn't know why Winter was saying this, but then he realized Winter had heard him while lost in his coma. As he left the pool room with Winter in his arms, relief coursed through him. He'd been right about one thing. Love did, indeed, conquer all, even death.

Chapter Nine

A few days later

"I suppose all's well that ends well," Winter said thoughtfully. "Uncle signed an agreement with the Cunninghams and invited them to the island. Now that we're here, Chantay was healed of the shadow curse, and so was Shea. Both of them seem to like life at the Sidhe palace a lot. Cherise is undergoing mental treatment. Uncle wanted to kill her, as she attacked a member of the royal family, but it seems she's not quite right in the head. She's not even pregnant. Either way, as long as she stays away from me and Corbin, I'm happy with it."

Winter looked at the silent monuments that marked his parents' resting place. He knew they weren't really there, as their souls and magic had long ago left their bodies. But sometimes, when he came here, he thought that he could feel their presence and sense their love.

"Corbin's been great," he continued. "I really wish you could have met him." He smiled fondly as he remembered his mate's overprotectiveness. "I'm sure you'd have loved him." He sighed and got up, gently caressing the letters of the engravings that read Lamont and Jayna Tomacelli. "I have to go now. He's waiting. But I'll be back soon. I'm teaching Corbin our world, so that he'll be ready when the time comes for us to lead the Sidhe people."

As he said his good-byes, Winter mused over the new discoveries of the past few days. Surprisingly, most fae had taken the news of his mating quite well. Perhaps Winter's near death had put things in perspective, or maybe Elder Mercier's fuck up had told them that it was time for a new policy toward shifters. Either way, while many seemed somewhat reluctant to believe a lynx could lead a fae nation, they'd been helpful and respectful.

Winter didn't kid himself. Those here might accept Corbin because he was Winter's mate, but other Sidhe who lived all over the world would not be so open-minded. Still, Winter trusted that he and Corbin could deal with any potential problem when the time came.

For the moment, though, Winter still had many questions, one of them being how his uncle had known what would happen to him and that Chantay could help. Sterling had refused to give them any explanation, just telling them that they had to be patient until the day came for them to lead the Sidhe nation.

In the end, some things couldn't be helped, and Winter knew all too well that when his uncle decided on something, trying to make the other man change his mind was akin to folly. With that in mind, Winter headed out of the sacred grounds and found Corbin waiting outside. They'd come here together, but his mate had decided to give him a few moments alone with his parents.

"Ready to go?" Corbin asked.

Winter nodded. "Come on. I want to show you around a bit more."

Hand in hand, they left the temple grounds and headed out of the palace. With everything that had happened, Sterling had insisted on Winter and Corbin having escorts at all times. As much as Winter had tried to convince his uncle otherwise, Sterling had been adamant. Sadly, this meant that Winter and Corbin couldn't stop by on the beach for an illicit romp, something Winter had been looking forward to.

"We don't need the beach to have fun together, sweetheart," Corbin purred in his mind.

Suddenly, Winter lost interest in sightseeing. His people weren't the only ones who'd gained perspective due to his near death. Winter himself had realized how much he was missing because of his fears.

He wished now that he could indeed offer Corbin the child the lynx wanted so much because that would truly make their family complete.

"We'll see about adopting later on, sweet," Corbin replied. *"For now, let's just enjoy each other, okay?"*

"I like that idea." Winter allowed his mate to lead him back toward the main palace grounds. They did their best not to hasten the pace, aware of all the eyes on them and the necessity of keeping a dignified posture.

Finally, after what seemed like forever, they reached the family wing. Winter's apartments were severely guarded even when he wasn't there, and the soldiers at his door bowed lowly in front of him. "At ease," Winter told them.

They slipped past the guards and into their bedroom. As a prince, Winter had lavish quarters, a huge apartment with its own receiving room and study, two baths, and of course, a richly decorated bedchamber. Once he became king, he would have a separate wing for his own use. Personally, Winter had never seen the point of so much luxury, but he appreciated the space for one particular reason. It prevented the guards at the door from hearing too much of Winter's cries when Corbin fucked him.

Corbin chuckled darkly, having obviously caught onto the thought. "If you're not screaming loud enough, it's obvious that I'm not doing my job right."

The lynx took Winter in his arms and carried him to the bed. In spite of his teasing words, Corbin's expression was one of concern. Lately, he always treated Winter as if he were made of glass. Not that Winter blamed him. Their bond told him how much Corbin had suffered when Winter had been at death's door. But at the same time, Winter wanted to leave all that behind. He wanted to begin a new life for the two of them and for the Sidhe people. And they hadn't made love since the time they'd been together on the Cunninghams' private island. Winter was going crazy with need.

"So am I, sweetheart," Corbin told him. "So am I."

Winter watched as his mate started to remove his shirt. It was silver, a royal garb specially sewn for Corbin as his position of future king-consort warranted. But as much as he admired his people's craft, it was the sight of the gorgeous body the outfit hid that left Winter breathless.

He licked his lips as Corbin revealed his strong chest. He wanted to lick across Corbin's tight abs and rub his body against the light feathering of hair on Corbin's chest. He ached for Corbin's possession, for his touch and claiming.

Without paying the slightest heed to the delicate material covering his own body, Winter rushed to get rid of his own clothing. His urgency fueled Corbin's, and the lynx helped him with his footwear and pants. Once Winter was naked, Corbin toed off his own shoes and unbuttoned his slacks, allowing them to pool down at his feet.

Now, both of them were naked and panting with desire. Corbin joined Winter on the bed, his larger body looming over Winter's. "Are you sure you're ready for this?"

"Are you kidding?" Winter hooked a naked leg against Corbin's midsection. "If you don't fuck in the next couple of minutes, I'm gonna die."

Corbin's expression darkened. "Don't joke with that, sweetheart. I don't think I can take it."

An apology was on Winter's lips. Even if he hadn't meant the words literally, he should have been more sensitive to his mate's feelings. But talk was useless between them. Their bond allowed their emotions to be expressed without being verbalized. As such, Winter pulled Corbin into a kiss, pouring his regret, need, lust, gratitude, and most of all, his love, into the lip-lock.

Corbin didn't delay in responding, taking control of the meeting of mouths, devouring Winter. Their tongues entangled, and Winter wrapped his arms around Corbin's neck, not wanting even the smallest space between them. His cock was so hard it could carve diamonds, and when Corbin reached between them and fisted the shaft, Winter cried out in pleasure. Already, he was very close to coming. In the weeks he'd spent together with Corbin, his body had become accustomed to regular sex, and the days he'd been forced to do without had been very difficult. He teemed with sexual tension just begging to come out, and he knew he would not last too long under his mate's skilled touch.

"Let go, sweetheart," Corbin whispered in his mind. *"We have all the time in the world."*

They didn't, but Winter wanted to believe it was true, regardless. He pushed aside the part of him that remained rational and focused solely on his mate. Corbin broke their kiss, his dark blue eyes fixed on Winter's face. "That's it, Winter. It's just the two of us now."

"Fuck me, Corbin," Winter whispered back. "Please, fuck me."

Corbin shook his head. "I won't fuck you," he replied, stressing the vulgar word. "I'll make love to you."

The lynx held Winter's gaze as he reached for the nightstand. Winter's heart raced with the anticipation, the sound of the uncapping of the lubricant bottle triggering an almost Pavlovian effect in him.

"Close your eyes, sweetheart," Corbin urged him. "Just feel."

Winter loved to meet Corbin's gaze as the other man fucked him, but there was something to be said about depriving himself of one of his senses. When he couldn't see, everything else seemed sharper, brighter. His nerve endings were more sensitive and Corbin's scent even more potent.

So Winter obeyed and closed his eyes, surrendering to whatever Corbin wished to do to him. Slick fingers probed at his nether opening while Corbin's mouth traveled over Winter's chest. Winter suppressed the urge to rush Corbin along and bit the inside of his cheek to push his impending climax back. He wanted this to last. He wanted to come only when he was impaled on Corbin's prick.

His mate released a sound that seemed like a cross between a growl and a purr. As Corbin's mouth now lingered over Winter's nipples, the vibrations caused shocks of pleasure to course through Winter. He arched his back, seeking more of the addicting sensations.

Corbin chuckled and flicked his tongue over the tiny nubs, then bit down, teasing Winter with just the right amount of pleasure-pain. Winter couldn't have suppressed his cries to save his life. "Corbin! Please...Please!"

His mate answered his plea by licking down his abdomen up to his navel. As Corbin thrust his tongue into the tiny hole, he also pressed two fingers inside Winter's ass, stretching him and readying him for invasion. Winter wanted to say he didn't need so much prep, but he knew Corbin would always be careful with him. It was just the way the lynx was, and Winter loved that about him.

At the same time, their bond guaranteed that Corbin never misinterpreted Winter's desires. Even as Winter struggled to control his desires, Corbin anticipated them. This time was no different. All of a sudden, the lynx lowered his mouth over Winter's prick and started to purr.

Distantly, Winter thought that having a feline lover truly brought some advantages. If the vibrations had felt good on Winter's nipples, around his cock, they brought him a little closer to heaven. He was torn between the need to thrust into the wet cavern of Corbin's mouth and the yearning to be filled that urged him to impale himself on Corbin's fingers. His mate didn't even give him the choice. Corbin crooked his fingers inside Winter, massaging Winter's prostate, just as he increased the suction on Winter's prick. It was all she wrote. Winter exploded, the climax sweeping through him and wiping away all rational thought.

Corbin didn't even give him time to recover from the pleasure. Instead, he removed his fingers from Winter's ass and positioned his prick at his hole. In one slow, smooth thrust, the lynx slid home. Winter's body, completely relaxed from his orgasm, greedily opened up to the penetration. Winter felt that finally, all was right in the world. Even if he'd only come moments ago, his cock went rock hard again as he lost himself in the pleasure his mate provided.

Fortunately, his lover was done teasing. He pulled out of Winter and thrust back inside, his thick prick massaging Winter's inner walls and unerringly hitting his prostate. Sparks flew through Winter, the heat of Corbin's cock burning him up from the inside out. Their sweat-slicked bodies rubbed together, and they fell into a rhythm that was perfection incarnate. Over and over, Corbin fucked him, taking possession of Winter, body and soul.

Winter's blood boiled, and his every nerve ending sizzled with passion and desire. Through his bond with Corbin, he felt his own emotions echoing inside the lynx. He was so close now, so close to another climax he was sure would even surpass the first. He just needed one more thing, the culmination of their bond and the truest essence of their nature as mates.

No sooner had Winter thought this than Corbin complied with the silent demand. He bit down on Winter's neck, his canines embedding themselves in Winter's flesh. White-hot pleasure-pain rushed over Winter, and crying out his mate's name, he found his peak once again. His mate joined him in absolute pleasure, filling Winter's body with hot seed. Their joint climax seemed to go on and on, Winter feeling the ecstasy twice, both through his own senses and through Corbin's. In moments such as these, he and Corbin ceased to be two people. They were one, two souls united in the most perfect moment of all time. It was so powerful, so transcendental, that Winter's mind couldn't take it. For a few seconds, he blacked out, the nirvana so intense it pushed aside his very consciousness.

When he came to, Winter found his mate looking down at him with a concerned expression. "Are you okay, sweetheart?" Corbin asked.

Winter smiled lazily. "Better than okay." He'd never felt more alive, more loved than he did with Corbin, and for that, he would never cease to be thankful.

Visible relief flooded Corbin's face. He briefly left the bed and padded naked to the bathroom. Winter allowed himself the luxury to watch his mate's naked form. When the lynx returned, carrying a wet washcloth, Winter beamed at him. "Love you, Corbin."

Corbin smiled back as he returned to the bed. "I love you, too, sweet," he said, gently cleaning Winter's body with the cloth.

Winter still had many things to say and even more he wanted to do. He yearned to spend every possible moment in Corbin's company. But much to his dismay, he found his eyes drifting shut. His orgasms seemed to have drained him dry and sleep beckoned like a siren's call.

Corbin chuckled lightly and lay next to him. "Sleep, Winter," the lynx said. "I'll be right here when you wake up."

Winter might have protested, but his lover started purring. The comforting sound lulled Winter into slumber, and as he surrendered to it, only warmth and happiness reached out to him from his dreams.

Epilogue

The last time he'd been at such a party, Winter had been too happy for his impending marriage to be truly concerned about its political implications. Now, however, he was more than aware of it. In fact, all throughout the reception, he'd been unable to focus on anything else except the calamity failure could bring.

"Are you okay, sweetheart?" Corbin asked, his voice concerned. "You look pale."

"I'm fine," Winter shot back snappishly. He usually liked Corbin's protectiveness, but now it grated on his already strained nerves. He would soon be the leader of a nation, for crying out loud. He couldn't cling to Corbin all his life.

"Leader of a nation you might be, but you're still my mate," Corbin said in a chastising tone. "Come sit down. You've had a busy day. You deserve a breather."

A scathing reply was already on Winter's lips, but the elders from various nations were close by, probably watching them. Since he'd recovered, he'd received several messages, not only from the vampires and the mer, but also from other species, who explained their concerns with recent developments in the paranormal society.

Elder Mercier's attack was only a symptom of a larger problem. She believed shifters were to blame for the conflicts between human hunters and magical creatures. Personally, Winter thought she was full of shit. Humans were the least of the Sidhe's problems. The never-ending battle between the Seelie and the Unseelie was much riskier, and the last thing they needed was foolish purism causing dissension. Regardless, some of the other species shared similar opinions, if not exactly to such an extent. And while Cherise's attack had been caused by what appeared to be a mental disorder, Winter had no doubt that the woman held resentment toward magical creatures as well.

Winter grimaced as a wave of queasiness flowed over him. To his knowledge, Sidhe couldn't get an ulcer because of stress, but maybe he was an exception. He'd certainly been feeling strange enough these days. His magic was erratic, his moods volatile, and his temper snappish. How could he help in building a better diplomatic future if he interpreted any comment as hostile?

Corbin was right. He needed a break. Sighing, Winter allowed his mate to lead him away from the group. Thankfully, Skylar and Sterling were around, and Winter knew they'd keep everyone busy long enough for him to take a breather.

"Have you eaten today?" Corbin inquired as Winter sat down on a nearby couch.

The nausea returned with a vengeance just at the thought of a meal. "I ate enough," he lied, knowing Corbin would see right through him. Sometimes, the mate bond had disadvantages, too.

Now was one of those times. Winter could have been snappish and annoyed had Corbin berated him angrily, but the lynx just gave him a concerned look. "Sweetheart, you have to eat. Please. You're really worrying me."

"Fine." Winter released a disgruntled sigh. "I'll try. For you."

Winter got up, intending to go to the buffet table and grab a small snack. He didn't get to reach his destination. He swooned, tripped, and would have had a painful meeting with the hardwood floor had Corbin not been there to catch him.

"That's it, Winter. I'm taking you upstairs, and I'm getting a medic to see you."

Winter wanted to protest being babied with so many important leaders close by, but he admitted he felt off. It wouldn't be a bad idea to get a healer to examine him. He was beginning to have some wild thoughts, and that sort of thing simply wouldn't do.

As if by miracle, his uncle materialized by his side, a wide smile on his face. Chantay followed in his tracks, quiet as always. "Well, then, I guess congratulations are in order," Sterling said.

"What?" Corbin asked, sounding shocked and a bit angered. "He's sick. The spell must be making a comeback or something."

Sterling shook his head, chuckling. "No. Nothing like that. Come now, Winter. Surely you must suspect what's going on."

The somewhat stoic Chantay smiled as well. Since recovering from the shadow curse, he'd been spending a lot of time with the Sidhe, learning about his heritage. Even if, in the beginning, he'd kept his distance from almost everyone, he seemed to be opening up now. If Winter wasn't mistaken, Elder Kevin Wade's son, Isaac, might have something to do with that.

"Don't look so put out, Your Highness," Chantay said. "This is a moment of joy."

Winter gaped at the two men, wondering how his uncle always seemed to know everything. "It's silly," he said, dismissing his own ideas before they could really compute. "There's no way it could happen."

But the thought had already flashed through his mind and must have slipped through his bond with Corbin. The lynx turned toward Winter, his eyes wide. "Pregnant?" he cried out.

Winter had never heard Corbin's voice sound so high pitched. It was funny, and he barely managed to suppress a hysterical giggle. "It's just a possibility," he replied.

"It's a certainty," Sterling corrected. "I can assure you that you are, indeed, carrying the next heir of the Sidhe throne."

Winter had always known that once upon a time, centuries in the past, Sidhe males had been able to give birth. But to his knowledge, that ability had gradually disappeared until Sidhe reproduction was strictly through heterosexual intercourse. Same-sex relationships weren't frowned upon, but for important families, the issue presented a problem.

He'd thought that, once he and Corbin were ready, they'd just adopt. Apparently, that wouldn't be necessary. But how could this happen? His mind whirled with shock, excitement, and just a little disbelief.

"Those abilities are still preserved among great healers, especially those of the royal line," Sterling explained. "I expect the healing process you underwent because of the spell might have made you even more fertile."

"So, you're sure then?" Corbin's voice was weak. "Winter's pregnant?"

"Oh, absolutely. Congratulations. You're going to be a father."

"Congratulations, Your Highness," Chantay echoed.

There was no doubt in either of the two men, and in that moment, Winter knew his uncle was right. He was going to have a baby.

A strange sense of calm filled him, and he beamed at his mate. "A baby, Corbin. Our baby."

It was Corbin's turn to swoon and Winter's to catch the lynx. They fell together back on the couch, laughing and unable to keep their hands off each other. Winter was aware of all the eyes watching them, but he couldn't care less. He was too happy.

His mate's hand landed on his still-flat stomach. "Thank you, sweetheart. Thank you."

Even as Corbin expressed his gratitude, Winter knew the truth. He was the one who should be thankful. He'd come here with hidden intentions and had found a new family and a mate who adored him. He'd gotten a second chance at life and managed to make his peace with his uncle. And now, the Nameless One had blessed him with a miracle, granting him the ability to fulfill Corbin's greatest wish, and yes, his own. Things might not be perfect, but he had his family, a family who loved and trusted him. What more could he wish for?

THE END

WWW.SCARLETHYACINTH.WEBS.COM

ABOUT THE AUTHOR

A native Romanian, Scarlet was born in 1986 and grew up an avid fan of Karl May and Jules Verne, reading fantasy stories and adventure. Later, when she was out of fantasy stories to read, she delved into her mother's collection of books and, of course, stumbled onto romance.

As a writer, though, Scarlet Hyacinth was born one sunny summer day, when a dear friend of hers—the same friend who introduced her to GLBT fiction—proposed they start writing a story of their own. As it turns out, the two friends never did finish that particular story, but Scarlet discovered she had a knack for writing and ended up starting to write individually. And so, between working on her dissertation, studying for exams, and reading yaoi manga, she started writing the Kaldor Saga. Along the way, Scarlet met a lot of wonderful people who supported her, and in the end, she found her story a home and, in the process, fulfilled a beautiful dream.

Also by Scarlet Hyacinth

Siren Publishing, Inc.
www.SirenPublishing.com

Lightning Source UK Ltd.
Milton Keynes UK
UKOW031903100912

198792UK00015B/254/P